ONE ANOTHER

ONE ANOTHER
A NOVEL
MONIQUE
SCHWITTER

Translated from the German by
TESS LEWIS

A KAREN AND MICHAEL BRAZILLER BOOK
Persea Books / New York

Originally published as *Eins im Andern* by Literaturverlag Droschl Graz (Austria) in 2015. First published in the English language by Persea Books in 2019.

Persea Books, Inc.
277 Broadway
New York, NY 10007

Library of Congress Cataloging-in-Publication Data

Names: Schwitter, Monique, 1972– author. | Lewis, Tess, translator.
Title: One another : a novel / Monique Schwitter ;
translated from the German by Tess Lewis.
Other titles: Eins im Andern. English
Description: First edition. | New York : Persea Books, 2019.
Identifiers: LCCN 2018023501 | ISBN 9780892554973 (pbk. : alk. paper)
Classification: LCC PT2720.W58 E4613 2019 | DDC 833/.92—dc23
LC record available at https://lccn.loc.gov/2018023501

*The publisher gratefully acknowledges the support of the
Swiss Arts Council Pro Helvetia, which made this publication possible.*

Design and composition by Rita Lascaro. Typeset in Arno Pro.
Printed by TK

FIRST EDITION

What, where, when

And yet, even when intent on one thing, we
already feel the allure of another. Enmity
is our kin. Aren't lovers
always arriving at boundaries, one after another,
that had promised expanse, the chase and a home?

—RAINER MARIA RILKE, *FOURTH DUINO ELEGY*

Clov: What is there to keep me here?
Hamm: The dialogue.

—SAMUEL BECKETT, *ENDGAME*

FOR YOU FROM ME

1

As fast as a person walks

When you suddenly google your first love, it's in response to the sound of knocking you hear just before you fall asleep and hear even louder the moment you look in the mirror in the morning and catch sight of the deep vertical crease between your eyebrows. You've tried, in vain, to locate the source of the knocking; it seemed to come now from inside, now from outside—up in the attic / inside your skull—but you could never pin it down.

The knocking comes more and more frequently, ever more inexplicably, and here it is again, this late Friday evening in January. As always, after a week in nursery school, the children were exhausted and overwrought; through the entire early evening they'd either been arguing or crying and later, because it was time for bed, they screamed like lunatics. They're finally asleep and for a moment it's completely quiet; even the dog is lying motionless on her blanket under my desk. I stare at her black fur until I can see her ribcage rise and fall. I breathe a sigh of relief and the knocking sets in, loud. Short, sharp hammer blows at first, which then alternate with longer blows. I draw dots and dashes in my notebook. Not that I know much about Morse code, but I study the chart until I can make out something halfway sensible. Halfway. SMOKE. TIME. KID. Well. (The alternatives were EUMOR. NATE. TEDD or IAOGN. TITN. NDNE. I don't know of any language in which those would make the slightest sense, and so I settle for *smoke, time, kid.*) Silence. My husband, I assume, is busy in his room working his way through the week's emails, something he does every Friday evening before calling out *weekend!* just before midnight. For a long time now, we've been planning on doing something together again. *Anything.* Sometimes he has no time, sometimes I don't. Smoketimekid! flits through my mind. I snap my notebook shut, and on the computer, open a new window. In the search box I type Petrus, the name of my first love.

I'm prepared not to find a single thing and to give up, resigned. I'm also ready for references to a wife and kids. Why shouldn't he have started a family by now? I am even prepared for photographs. But not for this. Not this. Still, Petrus had alluded to it on the first night we met. He had talked of flying, something humans can't do and how profoundly sad that made him. He started talking about falling and then quite suddenly changed the subject to walking; and because I asked: Walking? he added: Just one step, one single step into the void and it's all good. He spread his arms as if he wanted to fly, looked at me and smiled.

My husband walks into the room without knocking or saying my name, which rarely happens, only when we're fighting, when he's really angry, in a rage, or completely beside himself. Are you busy? he asks. No, I say and swallow the rest: I just learned about Petrus's death.

You're out of breath, he says.

Yes, I—I have no idea why, I'm just sitting here.

Maybe that's the reason.

He hesitates. He looks like he wants to say something. He takes a breath, looks away quickly and listens for something, for what, I have no idea. He starts to pull the door shut behind him.

Did you want something? I ask, but he answers, nothing that can't wait. He closes the door.

I open the drawer with the postcards and find what I'm looking for right away. An enormous, bearded St. Christopher in a brown cloak with disproportionately long legs and a tiny, doll-like Savior on his shoulder. On the back it says: *Depiction of St. Christopher (ca. 1400) in the St. Peter Mistail Church.*

I run my finger over St. Christopher's cloak, grab onto one of its brown folds, close my eyes and let myself be carried away. Back to that first time. It's winter, our first winter together. Petrus and I are visiting Marc's parents over the Christmas holidays in 1992, at their vacation home in the mountains.

Snowflakes fall, depending on their wetness, as fast as a person walks. I don't have winter boots and certainly no shoes that would be suitable for a long walk in the snow. I've got on the pumps I wear all year long—for miles, even if my feet hurt. It doesn't snow in the university.

Elfi looks at my shoes. Child, do you have any idea where you are? I nod, Lenzerheide. Elfi's son, Marc, and *his* Lisa are in the same seminar as I am and they also wear the same shoes every day and everywhere, but unlike mine, theirs are hiking shoes. Here, now, on the front porch of the vacation home, they have pulled on knee-high snow boots. Freshly oiled and with extra lining, Marc explains, eyeing my pumps. I'll just stay here then, I say and glance at the fire in the fireplace, the rattan rocking chair and the sheepskin Elfi draped over it, and at Urs—that's what I call him since I've forgotten his name—who, immersed in his history book, doesn't hear a word we're saying. He is sitting in his black leather chair, the book on his lap, and every now and then he pushes his glasses up onto his forehead, where his hairline used to be. But they keep slipping back down. *The Idea of Switzerland: Identity—Nation—History 1291–1991.* He was given the book as a Christmas present last year. Marc suspects he is memorizing it. Today is December 31st. Early afternoon. This evening, there will be fondue.

But first you've got to earn it, Elfi says and takes her crossword puzzle book and reading glasses from the sideboard.

Earn? I think of money because I don't have any.

Yes, Elfi says, with a walk to St. Peter's in Mistail. She wants us out of the house, her son translates for me, hugs his Lisa and kisses her passionately. Petrus takes his down jacket from the wooden peg and puts it on. He squats and ties his Timberland boots. He gave me a small book for Christmas. *Dialogue in the Void.* It's in English. I'll need time and a dictionary to read it. Come with us, Petrus says. My eyes turn to the fireplace. The sheepskin is alluring. There's a dictionary on the bookshelf across the room. Come on, Petrus says, they don't want you here. Elfi swats at him with her puzzle book. You're impossible, I never said that!

Elfi gazes up at Petrus who is over six feet tall. Her Urs, who may well have a different name—but not very different—is only five and a half feet tall. Her son Marc is just an inch taller than his father and she is two heads shorter than Petrus. You're someone to look up to, she says slowly and solemnly, leaning her head back and closing her eyes. Petrus comes from an old, wealthy family with a fortune only their closest circle knows the extent of and a family tree that can be traced back more than seven hundred years. Elfi had sensed it *immediately,* as she would say later. Nooo! Really? she exclaimed when she found out from her son, who outed their guest at our first dinner together with: Born rich, this one. Petrus opened his mouth, stared at his bread and cheese without a word, took a bite and chewed it thoroughly. They all looked at me. I was meant to confirm it. I took a gulp of Elfi's cloudy homemade apple juice and pretended to choke on it. Petrus had never offered me money for warm clothes or shoes. And I never would have accepted.

Come on already! Petrus, Marc and his Lisa call in chorus, ready to go out. And, after setting her puzzle book down on the sheepskin, Elfi presses a pair of sealskin boots into my hands and says: Here, these will keep you warm and snug. Sealskin! Like the ones our mothers supposedly wore in the seventies. Silvery and shimmering, real sealskin boots!

Too small, I tell her.

Thirty-eight, Elfi says.

I wear a thirty-nine.

Elfi: They run big.

Everyone watches in anticipation as I stick my right foot into the sealskin boot and before I've even zipped it up, they say: They'll do. You see. Wonderful. Too tight, I say but Petrus, Marc, and Lisa are already outside. They're throwing snow at each other, and Elfi says in parting: You really don't need such thick socks, the boots are warm enough. She closes the door. A snowball hits me right in the left eye, I see flashes, I hear thunder, then Petrus yells: Sorry! and lobs the next one in my direction. Hep, hep— Marc claps his hands. Let's move! Petrus reaches me in a few long strides, grabs me and throws me over his shoulder. What on earth did you eat? he groans. You weigh at least a ton. Marc carries his Lisa piggyback and neighs as he gallops away with her.

Panting under his ton, Petrus hurries after them down the small lane to the village street, throws his head back and, barely two hundred meters from the crossroad, he collapses dramatically, dropping me on my back and landing heavily on top of me. We both moan. Where is this church? I ask and Petrus laughs. Marc, we yell together, is it still far?

No, no, Marc says and adds that it's worth the few kilometers walk, the church is unique.

A few kilometers?

Don't worry, he walked there when he was only five, he reassures us, it's a pleasant stroll uphill.

My feet hurt. The sealskin boots are too short and too narrow. Even with the zipper undone, my feet feel like they're being squeezed in steel vices. On my instep I can feel my pulse hammering hard against the unyielding leather. We've pushed our way forward along the main road of Lenzerheide village, past all the hotels and sporting goods stores, in a column of hundreds of winter sports enthusiasts, wearing ski boots and carrying skis on their shoulders. Whenever one of them turned around, his skis would hit the person in front or behind in the head. This was followed by swearing or laughter, occasionally both, one right after the other. We kept silent. I stayed close behind Petrus, my eyes glued to his heels, and I counted out each step with gritted teeth, as if it might take some of the pressure off my feet. After the village limit, Marc led us further up a smaller road to a dairy farm, where the watchdog barked furiously and lunged against his chain, working himself into a frenzy. Behind the farm, we reached the hiking trail.

A rest. I grab Petrus's sleeve for support, but he drops to his knees without a word and offers me his back. After a determined hop, I wrap my arms around him from behind, until he says, *No choking, please.* And Lisa says, *Brr, brr, whoa. Stand still, horsey.* Marc obeys and lets her climb on his back.

The men wished hiking were more popular so the trails would be better worn. With us on their backs, they sank, side by side, up to their knees in the snow with every step. After just a few meters they were already staggering from the effort, but they still managed to carry us past the lumber mill and the carpenter's shop, past the golf course and all the way to the mountain pasture, where the path turned abruptly into the forest. I can't anymore, Petrus says. Finally, Marc answers. They groan as they set us on the ground at the forest edge and stretch out spread-eagle on the snow. I want to take off the sealskin boots to check my feet, which I can no longer feel. Don't do that, Petrus says, you'll never get them back on. Then he winks and lifts his arm toward the sky. Snow is starting to fall.

We could no longer make out the path in the forest above the mountain pasture. The snow was deep, icy, and perforated from rain showers during the day and frost at night. We broke through the surface with a crack and sank up to our hips, and the snow was compacted into ice under the weight of our steps. I managed exactly 123 steps, then I tore the boots from my feet, pulled them over my hands and walked on in damp socks, my feet numb but liberated. The first few steps were the most pleasant I've ever taken in my life. I kept counting out of habit and again stopped at 123. The cold was making my feet even more numb than the pain had.

I tried to wiggle my toes but couldn't feel any movement aside from a painful throbbing that shot up my legs in waves and almost made my knees buckle. We're just about there, Marc yelled from a distance and Petrus, who had stopped a few steps ahead of me, yelled back: Admit it, Marc, you have no idea where we are!

Marc yelled back that he has known this forest since he was a kid, the snow won't confuse him, he could find the way blindfolded.

Petrus turned to face me. It's beautiful! Come over here, let's sit down. He smiled gently. I looked at him and, as so often, I didn't know if he was joking or not. We'll just stay here. He collapsed into the snow as if hit by a bullet. Lie down close to me! It won't take long before you don't feel the cold anymore, you'll see. Marc and Lisa had gone on ahead and were already out of sight. After a while, Petrus stopped answering me. I heaved myself up, lunged toward him in my icy socks, grabbed his hand, pulled him onto his feet and dragged him behind me through the lightly falling snow, following the deep, vertical footsteps that Marc and Lisa left behind, even though I wasn't really convinced they would lead out of the forest and eventually back to somewhere warm. The right boot must have slipped from my hand on the way. I only noticed it was missing when we were standing, what seemed hours later, in front of the St. Peter Mistail Church.

Marc jiggled the church door. He threw himself against it. With a stream of threats and curses—he had an impressive number of both in his arsenal—he went at the door until his arms hurt so much he had to stop. Lisa stared blankly at the ground. I tried to catch Petrus's eye; he was standing off to the side, watching attentively. Then, with the authority of someone four years older, he slapped Marc on the back. Come with me! Let's see if—

If? Marc rubbed his forearm.

If there's a window open somewhere, Petrus said.

What nonsense, a church window left open, Marc groused in response. But he started to move anyway. We followed Petrus around the church. The snow was now falling in thick flakes, landing heavily on our hats and, after a few moments, it had turned us into a group of grizzled seniors. Petrus, as was fitting, looked like the oldest and most distinguished because he had a hat with ear flaps and a scarf over his face, and they turned into a head of white, wavy hair and a stately full beard. Petrus the apostle, I said. Fat granny, he shot back.

We stand before a chapel-like extension and peek through an opening at hundreds—I start counting—thousands of carefully stacked bones, femurs and skulls, bare, clean, and tidy, like the perfectly arranged piles of firewood you see in front of every house here.

What we are now, you will become, what you are now, we once were is written on a wooden sign propped up in the middle of the bones.

A bone house, Petrus whispers. Take a look at that.

You don't need to whisper, they can't hear you anymore, Marc says in an intentionally loud voice, and they both laugh.

I reach for Petrus's hand. My feet! Can we go now?

Lisa stares at my socks in horror.

It's all fine, I say, I just can't feel anything.

Elfi let me know through Urs how upset she was about the lost boot. She had retreated to the kitchen to prepare the cheese fondue and didn't want to be disturbed. In the meantime, we were to set the table, get the chafing dish ready, and cut the bread into small pieces. Among the five of us we got it all done very quickly and then stood around the table, embarrassed. Urs cleared his throat: Elfi is very upset that the boot is lost.

I'm really very sorry, I said.

What is she supposed to do with a single boot? Ridiculous, a shoe without a mate, useless, superfluous, pointless.

Marc listened to his father attentively and nodded after *ridiculous* and *mate*.

I nodded, too, with my eyes on Petrus, who was trying to stifle a yawn. In vain. It's the warmth, he apologized, and the *Kaffee Luz.*

But Urs didn't hear him. Those boots cost a small fortune at the time. I gave them to her, hang on, twenty-three years ago, as a present, yes, the first time we ever came up here together. Urs beamed and suddenly couldn't continue.

Petrus was yawning again. He had downed four glasses of the coffee with schnapps, served boiling hot, in an inn not far from the church while Lisa and I both had alternated between blowing on and taking sips from our first cups. Without paying any attention to his drink, Marc had gnawed the knuckles of his fist and hissed to himself. He was calling some invisible person a *goddamn moron,* a *phenomenally stupid hayseed from Hell,* the *brainless spawn of darkness.* Finally, he sat up, breathed deeply in and out, picked up his glass, and drained it. Then he smiled. Another?

Petrus had nodded, but Lisa objected, it's already getting dark and high time we started back. Sensation was gradually returning to my feet, first my toes tingled, then little prickles started pelting my feet faster and faster from all sides until finally an excruciating internal pressure set in and my feet felt like they were going to explode. I looked out the window into the twilight. The streetlamps had been lit. Heavy snow flurries. It looked like the snowflakes were swirling upward, from the pavement to the sky. Petrus had gotten to his feet and settled the bill with the waitress behind the massive wood bar. She shook her head several times and laughed, then she said: Yes, sure! Sure!

When Petrus returned to the table, he put the post card in front of me. There weren't any of the bone house, unfortunately, he said, but here, St. Christopher. We'd have seen him if the church hadn't been closed. He lay his hand on my shoulder. It's unusual to see his portrait inside a church because the sight of him guards against death, that's why he's often painted on outside walls. Petrus drew his finger along St. Christopher's cloak. He's a good six meters tall.

I flipped the card over. How do you know that?

I just do.

And he carries on his shoulders—

The weight of the world.

Isn't that the young Jesus?

Yes.

Marc and Lisa had stood up and were ready to leave. Petrus stayed in his chair. He had ordered a taxi, he told us, and another round of schnapps.

Urs had finished his book. Elfi had solved all the puzzles in hers. They'd been worried. Elfi even called the police, but they were unfazed and wished her a happy New Year. Elfi and Urs had sat in front of the fireplace and listened for us, for hours, until Urs's lower eyelid twitched and Elfi's hands fluttered. Elfi had screamed when we came through the door, and we flinched in fright.

When the taxi driver had finally arrived at the inn, he explained he'd forgotten us. By the time he remembered, he'd already quit for the day and had to get dressed again. Now I'm here. So much new snow had fallen that he probably should have put his chains on. But, he added, for this last ride of the year, it wasn't worth it. Please get in.

I have no memory of the ride. But I do remember Elfi's scream. And the look on her face. The disappointed look she gave Petrus as she passed us without a word on her way to the kitchen, where, according to her messenger, Urs, she wanted to prepare the fondue without distraction.

The evening was well advanced by the time we gathered at the table and dunked bits of bread in the cheese. We washed down each bite with a small glass of Kirsch. Elfi did not say a word before midnight. When the church bells rang, she sprang up and said Happy New Year! and gave everyone a hug, even me, despite the lost boot. Then she put on a yellow turban and informed us that she would now look into our futures. She saw us there as couples, saw our happy children, and somewhat more distantly, but still clearly, she assured us, she even saw our grandchildren. Petrus smiled, and Elfi blew him a kiss. And thus the evening and the year ended.

Later, Marc locked his Lisa out of their house—they were married by then. It was jealousy. He claimed she was having an affair with her dermatologist, whom she saw weekly for her eczema. Not long after, Lisa claimed Marc had raped her. She left him, at which point—and I'm not the only one bothered by this—she first moved in with his parents, Urs and Elfi. There were no children. (But I only learned all this secondhand.)

I left Petrus a year after the New Year's in Lenzerheide, in autumn, after my friend Katrin told me one cool July day that he had cheated on me with her more than a year earlier. Granted, I had also cheated on him. But the thing with Katrin, that was betrayal, I decided. Afterward, we still heard from each other for a while, but less and less. He needed distance, he said, and I found that convenient.

One of the children has started crying. Let's see if I can hold out until my husband leaves his room, turns on the flashlight, and goes to check. The dog crawls out from under the desk and looks at me reproachfully. I'm not deaf, I say. I try to ignore both the dog and the crying. In the hallway, I bump into my husband. I got it, he says. Good, I answer. He turns left into the children's room, I turn right and return to my office. I read what I've written. I look outside. It's snowing. I picture Petrus in the open window on the ninth floor.

On the night we met, at the kitchen table of the mutual friend who'd introduced us—with a hidden agenda, as she later revealed—Petrus had already dropped a hint: As soon as I can go, I will.

Where?

Away.

Where?

And that's when he spread his arms and smiled.

2

No, not like that. More like this.

The first thing that occurs to me is to write to Andreas. That's what I call him since he's Petrus's brother and *Andreas* fits. ~~I only just found out. My heartfelt condolences.~~ No. ~~My deepest symp~~ No. ~~I was trying to get in touch with Petrus and learned that~~ No, not like that. More like this:

I had a sudden longing for old times. When I googled Petrus's name, I came across the entry: *Public figure. Was a German historian, publisher, and professor.* Was.

Died on November 17, 2008. More than four years ago! When I was pregnant. I had just become pregnant, finally, and my previous life—with never enough sleep, rest, or care taken, but no scarcity of alcohol, coffee, and cigarettes—was over. It was very hard for me to go forward: the nicotine withdrawal was hell. I found myself in a never-ending dialogue with cigarettes and the baby, the baby and cigarettes. I didn't long for anyone— except the baby. I didn't miss anyone—except the cigarettes. I couldn't think clearly. I couldn't write anymore. Intellectual life without cigarettes didn't seem possible. Did I want that kind of a life?

That was when Petrus decided to jump out of a ninth-story window. He is gone and I hadn't noticed. How can the news of someone's death be so upsetting if you haven't missed him for years?

It's ridiculous to send Andreas condolences four years after his brother's death, but after a rough night filled with vague attacks of longing, I search for his address.

I type Andreas's name into a few search engines and social networks. He seems to be alive, director of some—what exactly?— large Scottish bank. Chief Risk Officer. I picture him, from bottom to top, in handmade semi-brogues, a slim-fitting tailored cashmere suit with a silk tie and matching pocket square, smooth shaven, and bald, of course, as he was even then. Just a second. I blink: now he's got on knee-high, pitch-black rubber boots with thick soles and a wide shaft; an old, stained pair of brown pants; a large-checked flannel shirt, and carries a gun. A gun? Yes, he aims the barrel in turn at his brothers then at me, and a salvo of hissing, crackling, and snapping sounds flies out of his mouth until he has to laugh—all alone—so insanely that his mouth is no longer any kind of muzzle and he leaves us alone. And his lips? What do they look like after so many years? I search under *images,* but don't find anything. And yet, it keeps getting bigger. But what is spreading out before me is no longer an upper lip, not even a badly stitched up, hastily treated, thickly scarred one. What keeps expanding in front of me is something else, an unloved, actually long-destroyed, shredded story whose scraps and tatters are banding together, piling up, towering over me—and forming hideous new aspects and grimaces.

Suddenly it was summer. We woke up dazed and couldn't explain where the morning mugginess had come from. The spring had been a very rainy one, the shrubs and trees had leafed out as if for the last time; this was no delicate shade of color, but a deep, untamed green that threw thick shadows. Petrus stroked my back with the duck feather he used as a bookmark. My hand would stick, he said, let's swim. We rode along the riverbank on our bicycles, no-hands, under the trees through the hard, rapidly alternating bands of light and shade, so close to each other that our handlebars almost snagged, and Petrus said: In two weeks I have to leave. I immediately fell and split my knee open. To tend sheep in France, he added as he brushed gravel out of the wound with his hand. I gave him a dark look because I didn't believe him. The tenant farmer is taking his family vacation on the Atlantic coast and I agreed to fill in for him and take care of the farm like I did last year.

You never told me about that.

No? I thought I did.

I leapt up, grabbed my bicycle, jumped on it, and rode off as fast as I could. Petrus chased me. When he had almost caught me, he yelled: Not a chance! From the corner of my eye, I saw that he was about to pass me and I let go of the handlebars, sat up straight and shot my right arm straight out to the side like a barrier. Petrus yelped and fell, and then I had to clean his knee. And not only that: one of his elbows was scraped, his wrist bruised, his ankle sprained. You're not all there, he said and gave me a much darker look than I'd given him.

I'm sorry.

He didn't answer.

After swimming—despite his injuries, he did his three kilometers of crawl and I did my few lengths of breaststroke—he used the shower next to the pool, I used the one in the dressing room, he broke his silence at the exit turnstile, asking: Will you come with me?

Of course, I answered.

The farmer's vacation lasted four weeks. The sheep farm was in the middle of the middle of France, in the region that was home to the Bourbons, whose crest that *département* still bears, and bordered a forest the size of Paris, almost exclusively of oak—twenty-to-thirty meter tall sessile oak trees.

Petrus's mother was given the farm as a wedding present from her grandfather. One day Petrus and his brother would inherit it, along with many other seigneuries, agricultural and forestry holdings, fields, forests, and vineyards in Europe, Canada, and South Africa.

I spent the first week—hot days in early July—wandering around in borrowed, size forty-five black rubber boots, looking at the sheep in the stall until I had the feeling they were staring back at me. I pretended to be interested in the farm machinery and all the equipment lying around such a breeding station until Petrus made it clear that he could hear my internal yawning. Then I set off exploring the surroundings paths and pastures in my pumps, all the way to the nearby village with its original—but, to me, uninspired and squat—Romanesque church and once went on a daylong walk, barefoot, through the oak forest, where I got so completely lost that I was already preparing myself mentally to the idea that I'd be spending the night in immediate proximity to deer, wild boar, and tawny owls when a hiker terrified me by appearing suddenly and silently in front of me, and he then explained with gentle words and an astonishing repertoire of gestures and hand motions how to get to the village. An acrid smell of sweat streamed toward me as he raised his arms again and again, pointing in every possible direction. Each time I nodded and said, *Entendu, merci beaucoup, Monsieur,* he added additional, more complicated, arm-waving elucidations until I finally turned and hurried off. That seemed to be exactly what he was waiting for.

So much for the environs. The truth is that I didn't have any time for the forest and fields, the locals, or sheep since I had planned on using these four weeks to write my term paper on Beckett's dramaticule *Come and Go*, which consists of exactly 120 words on two pages, a manageable project, you'd think, even though the paper naturally had to be the usual required length of thirty pages despite the brevity of the work discussed. And that's where it got difficult. I intended nothing less than to give Beckett studies a fundamental boost with an astounding, yet compelling new interpretation. Even if I only had two semesters of study behind me. I was going to root out the riddle that Beckett posed for himself and for us, with this play, through sustained meditation. I spent entire mornings, entire afternoons searching for the key to this work by pacing throughout the house in my high heels, pacing from the kitchen to the bathroom to the bed or, barefoot, over the hot gravel in front of the house to the stone bench near the driveway, which very quickly became uncomfortable. Or I pulled on a pair of those enormous black size forty-five rubber boots, of which there were at least a dozen lying around, all of which seemed to belong to William, the tenant farmer, and I paced back and forth over the narrow strip of grass between the wall and the manure pile in big, shuffling steps. As I paced, I immersed myself in the master's few sentences and stage directions as if in an oracle. I'll get to the bottom of it, I told myself, nodding with each step and murmuring Beckett's text, conjuring, hands waving, until Petrus came out of the sheepfold and stopped me. He was accompanied, as always, by three shaggy dogs, border collies that were apparently exceptionally well-trained experts in their field, herding sheep. They came from the oldest and most highly regarded breeding center in Great Britain and therefore understood only English. *Lie down* was all I could say. *Lie down* was all I needed to communicate to these dogs, whom I didn't trust for a minute. As soon as one appeared, I would call out *lie down,* and he would immediately drop, even on the way to a full dog dish, fixing me with an expectant and—I have to admit—downright friendly look. I had no idea how to say *Get up and walk,* or *Do whatever you want,* or *Eat, for all I care.* So it was always Petrus who released the dogs with complicated commands I couldn't begin to understand, even though he swore he was speaking English. The dogs would rise, take a few steps, sit on their haunches, lift alternate paws and, after giving three short barks, they would trot over to the feeding dish, sit down politely, and wait. Petrus would praise them, speak to them for a while, and then give them permission to eat. When I asked what he said to them, he'd answer: I give them feedback, I tell them what they did well and how they can improve. And then he added *apropos,* and with this lovely French word, he turned to face me and looked intently at a spot between my eyebrows—he never looked me in the eye, but always between my eyebrows—and continued: You shuffle around in the shade and, like a potato, try to germinate on your own. That is extremely unscientific. Where are you getting your interpretation from? That is the essential and most fundamental question. What are you basing it on? An artist may find creative sparks within and create something from that, but scholars or scientists? Never. No, they would never get any- where that way.

What about Newton, I objected, didn't he discover gravity by looking at an apple tree? (I'm rarely quick with a comeback, the spark must have ignited my brain.)

Oh, Petrus retorted, I see, you're bringing out the big guns. Newton, well then, I am sorry to interrupt. I eagerly await your next explanation of the world, my esteemed Isaac. Then he said some- thing to the dogs that I didn't understand and walked off toward the stone bench, his steps crunching on the gravel. I watched him go, him and his matted, panting dogs, who circled him tirelessly, I saw him open the blue enamel mailbox and take out the newspaper along with an envelope, saw him slip the envelope into his pants pocket, sit down on the bench, and open the newspaper.

Night fell and the heat gradually let up. Put on some rubber boots and come to the stall with me, Petrus said, I want to show you something. He shut the dogs up in the house and took a large flash- light from the hook near the key rack next to the door. We walked single-file in silence to the stall. My bare feet slid around inside the enormous boots with every step, chafing first against the hard toe box then against the worn back. Before Petrus opened the door to the stall, he put his finger to his lips. He repeated the gesture emphatically and slid back the wooden latch. It was almost ten and dark inside. In response to our entry, a few lambs bleated. We heard rustling, scraping, and snorting. Then it gradually quieted down again. Petrus and I crouched down next to the door and tried to see each other in the darkness. I had fixed my eyes where I guessed his eyes were and he looked at the spot between my eyebrows, assuming he could locate it. The still of night. And then, out of nowhere, came a thundering roar like an avalanche of gravel pouring onto the metal roof directly over our heads. Over our heads? No, the hail seemed instead to be pattering down the wall next to us, no—was it possible?—to be pattering *up* the wall! What is that? I asked as soon as I got enough breath back. Petrus turned on the flashlight and shone it at the wall across from us. Rats! They scurried in chaotic masses over the untreated timber, without any obvious goal or definite direction. Then they seemed to be banding together in the eaves—what were they doing up there, what were they discussing? Then things quieted down. Did they have a plan? A renewed volley: with insane speed they scattered over the walls, tending downward this time, countless paws and claws drummed, beat on the wood. Dozens reached the floor of the stall: they ran, whirled around, crashed into each other, tumbled over one another. A few headed toward us. I leapt up, yanked open the stall door, and fled outside. Petrus followed me unhurriedly. Since the beginning of the warm season, they've multiplied exponentially, he said calmly. Their population seems to have reached its peak. I think we have to act.

We? I don't know the first thing about rats.

Petrus came up to me, took me in his arms, and said: No? We kissed and as soon as I closed my eyes it seemed to me that rats were dancing over my retina and making it flicker. My brothers are coming tomorrow, Petrus whispered into my ear, his breath tickling pleasantly, they're on their way home from Lacanau and will make a short stop.

I opened my eyes. Is that what the letter said? I asked.

He loosened his hug. Which letter?

Petrus had three brothers. From the back, all four of them looked the same. No matter that Petrus was the tallest, they all had the same physique, the same long torso, straight back, and sloping shoulders, the same short, strong legs. From the front, you would never confuse them. One bald, the other bearded, the third, well, pink. Andreas was twenty-seven, just two years older than Petrus and already almost completely bald. He had a narrow face with deep-set eyes that were constantly changing color. Blue. Gray. Green. His mouth seemed out of place, as if stolen from someone else's face: much too curved, too soft, too beautiful. He was studying business administration at the St. Gallen Hochschule, which was known for producing *assertive* managers.

The oldest, Joseph, lived in Canada, where he managed several forests owned by the family. Joseph rarely spoke. Petrus had told me he was desperately looking for a suitable woman to marry. But there were hardly any women in the Canadian forests and the few Joseph had met were out of the question.

Why's that? I wanted to know.

Why's that? I have no idea, Petrus replied.

In any case, Joseph didn't shave and had grown an unappealing, unkempt beard.

Martin, the youngest, seemed to put the most stock in his appearance. He wore pressed shirts, aftershave, and styled his hair with a gel that, perhaps because of the heat, smelled pungently of artificial peach. For all his twenty-three years, he looked sixteen, blushed constantly, never held anyone's gaze, and was prone to fits of laughter that made him sound like a young girl.

When their car, a station wagon with electronic music thundering from its windows, drove up to the house, the dogs leapt up, barking, and encircled it. The music was finally turned off but that didn't reassure the dogs. I watched the scene from the kitchen window. One of the brothers—from Petrus's description, I immediately recognized him as Andreas—rolled down the driver side window and said something to the dogs, who kept jumping up, almost to his face. I walked out of the kitchen, opened the door, and yelled: Lie down! The dogs fell silent, dropped to the ground, and stayed. Wow, said Andreas, what did you say to them?

Lie down—they only speak English.

Lie down, he repeated. Where's Petrus? he asked.

Where are Joseph and Martin? I asked in response and peered into the car. Joseph sat in the front passenger seat, looking at me silently and suspiciously. Martin lay curled up on the back seat and laughed. Did you bring your girlfriend? I asked. He fell silent and shook his head uncomprehendingly. Don't you want to get out? Martin started laughing again and Joseph gazed at me fixedly. And the dogs? Andreas asked softly, as if he were afraid of getting them worked up.

After Petrus had driven into the village to get beer and meat to grill, he handed them shirts and pants from the farmer's closet, told them to find themselves some rubber boots, and led them toward the stall. When I followed, more than an hour later, I found them sitting in the grass in front of the stall, in a wonderful mood and talking animatedly to each other. Lie down, Andreas called when he saw me. Martin squealed with delight and had laughing fit. The others also found this very amusing. Even Petrus—granted, he tried to hide his giggles, but I heard them. I got the joke only after thinking about it for a while. Petrus put his arm around me. He said, It's not easy to understand, but Andreas doesn't mean anything by it. Petrus sighed. Actually, he means it in a nice way. I looked over at Andreas. Lie down, he called out again and laughed until he shook, and his brothers laughed with him.

Are they spending the night here? I asked Petrus as he made the fire.

He gave me a questioning look.

Yesterday you said they were only stopping by.

Yes, he replied, but first we have to eat.

Andreas went to look at the stall. Martin spent an hour in the tub. Joseph stood at the grill without a word, looking darkly into the coals, and forgot to turn the steaks.

What did you do in Lacanau? I asked Joseph. They were surf-
ing, Petrus answered for him. You don't look like you had good
weather, I said having turned back to Joseph. We don't get tan
in our family, Petrus replied. And how is life in Canada? I tried
for a third time in Joseph's direction. Lonely, Petrus answered.
He looked at me and said: Let him be. It was his answer that was
indiscreet, not my question. I asked myself what the world would
come to if all younger brothers started defending their older
brothers.

Andreas came back from the stall. He was grinning. I found
a pitchfork, he said, but that's probably not the right implement.
Joseph shook his head. Petrus said: We can eat now.

A pungent scent announced Martin's return from the bathroom. Poison, he asked, have you considered poison?

We don't have any poison, Petrus answered.

And poison's no fun, Andreas added. Blow them away!

Yes, but with what?

There must be some kind of shotgun on the farm somewhere?

I already searched the entire stall, nothing.

Small bore would be the thing!

You guys remember Uncle Walter? He had a real rat-killer in
his closet, double-barreled with nine-millimeter pellets and a
twenty-two gauge LR cartridge. Reliable thing.

I'd be careful with the small bore, because of the ricochets,
much too dangerous.

A small-bore rifle with pellets would work, back in the day we
shot hundreds of pigeons from two to six meters away with one.

Bullshit, that wasn't a small bore, that was an air gun. Man,
those pigeons were disgusting, remember?

There are air guns here.

A moment of silence followed.

Are you serious? An air gun? No, really, that's anti-social.

How's that?

You'll wound them at best, but kill them? Forget about it.

They'll end up crawling around all shot up and bleeding, it's cruelty to animals.

Hello . . . they're rats!

For a while it hadn't been clear which of them was saying what. They stood in a small circle. I was behind them and it struck me again that they all looked alike.

They finally agreed to give the air gun a try. While Petrus went and got it, Andreas told us about an acquaintance named Annie who suddenly had an entire colony of rats on her property because of her neighbors, disgusting health food fanatics with their revolting compost heaps. Annie set her hunting terrier on the rats. It took care of twenty-seven of them in a single day, seven more the next day, and that was that. She never saw another rat. Andreas gave a short, sharp bark like a terrier, then looked at me and called: Lie down!

Petrus handed his flashlight to Andreas, who fastened it onto the barrel of the gun with a cable tie. He shouldered the gun and looked at his brother. Joseph nodded and took command. The four of them marched to the stall in single file, all wearing the same borrowed, ugly black rubber boots. When Joseph slid back the door bolt, Martin couldn't contain himself any longer and started giggling. His brothers grabbed him, pushed his head backward, and holding his mouth shut, dragged him into the barn, where they threw him onto the straw next to the tractor. The three of them went back without a word, slipped out of their rubber boots and tiptoed in stocking feet into the stall. I stood with one foot in the stall, one foot outside. Close the door, one of them called. The voice sounded unfamiliar, maybe Joseph's. We waited.

When the storm broke, the thousand-fold patter of rat paws on wood, Andreas turned on the flashlight and shot. Silence. They were gone. Andreas pointed the gun and the light at the floor. A single rat lay there. He went up to it, the gun ready. Did it hit you? he asked, sounding tender. He dropped to one knee to poke it. Nothing. It got hit, he said and bent lower to pick it up and show it to us. He reached for it with his free left hand, we couldn't see more than that, and a second later, Andreas screamed. The squirming rat hung from his upper lip. I turned on the overhead light. Andreas roared. He spun in a circle, grabbed at the rat with both hands and pulled. He screamed with pain, let go of the rat, and yelled, help me, you idiots, do something! He twitched and jerked and danced in a circled, and seemed to be losing his mind. Petrus tore the gun out of his hand and aimed at him. Are you insane? Andreas yelled. Hold still, I'll kill it, Petrus answered. Suddenly Martin was standing next to him. Don't shoot, do not shoot, he said. Martin, the little giggler, how did he get here? He, of all people, spoke calmly and firmly: Lie down, Andreas, lie down on your side, good, that's good. Andreas lay motionless. Martin held the rat tight and held it against the ground. Joseph grabbed the gun from Petrus and beat the rat to death with the butt. It took one, two, three, four, five blows. Andreas groaned with each blow, as if he were the one hit. The dead rat still hung fast to his lip. Wait, I'll break its jaw, Martin said, but Andreas pushed him away and, with a roar, tore the rat from his lip with his own hands.

Petrus handed me a small page from a notebook that the farmer had pinned to the kitchen cupboard. Here, he said, William told me that if we needed a doctor, we should call this number. *Didier 67587.* Didier was not very pleased with the late call. First, I talked at him, trying to explain the situation, then he at me: He was a vet, *vétérinaire, pas un médecin.* He gave me the number of some Joujou or Chouchou. I split the difference and wrote Shushu.

He couldn't believe it. *Un rat?* he kept repeating and then even tried it in English: A rat? *Oui,* I said, yes.

It took him more than an hour to arrive, during which time the brothers intensively cared for Andreas. One continuously dabbed away blood, one poured schnapps into him, one lay cold compresses on his forehead and the back of his neck. Only I sat drinking the beer—contrary to my usual habit—that they had brought back from the village that afternoon.

Shushu was completely taken with the wound. He spoke softly and very quickly to himself: That is really ugly, my God, very serious. Rat bites are always relatively dangerous because they also grind their jaws sideways when they bite. They really pierce the wound with their teeth, even if you can't tell from the outside, which naturally isn't the case here, the damage is on the inside, just take a look, here you can see it perfectly, completely shredded! You should be happy it isn't a human bite, as far as infections go, human bites are hell, but there might be some bacteria we don't like here, too, after all. Be careful. He gave Andreas a shot of painkiller and antibiotics, cleaned the wound and said: I have to take you with me. We'll decide in the hospital whether or not you need stitches.

Martin had fallen asleep on the sofa. Joseph stared blankly and drank the last bottle of beer. Petrus made himself a coffee and chewed his lower lip. I'd switched to schnapps and thought about Beckett. *Just sit together as we used to . . . One sees little in this light . . . May we not speak of the old days?* I remembered the letter and went to Petrus's bedroom to look for it. What time is it? Petrus asked when I came back. He answered the question himself after glancing at the pendulum clock in the hall: three- thirty. The letter you got today, where is it? I asked him. The letter, Petrus repeated and paused briefly, it wasn't for me. I put it on the table for William. Can I see it? Petrus looked at me between my eyebrows, concerned. See? I think you should go get some sleep, the sun will be up soon.

It's darkest night, a voice objected. Nobody move! Andreas appeared in the doorway, his arm aimed like a gun and behind it, the bandage, which had been wrapped around half of his head, almost disappeared. He was drunk, his arm trembled, he let it sink. Shushu is a good man, he said. Is there anything left to drink? He seemed old, not because he was bald. The way he stood there in the farmer's clothes, the shirt with its enormous brown checks, the dung-colored pants, he looked tired, exhausted.

Where's the rat? he asked. On the manure pile, I answered. Have you all gone crazy? he asked and went to the door. Turned around. And the gun? Here, Joseph said (Joseph said something!) and pulled the air gun out from under the sofa. He handed it to Andreas, who dropped onto an armchair and laid it across his knees. Does it hurt? I asked. He looked at me scornfully, much too long, he just didn't take his eyes off me. Give me a kiss, he said. Hey, Petrus objected, and laughed. Give me a kiss, Andreas repeated. A kiss, he said to Petrus, she can give me a kiss, right? No, no, Petrus said, still laughing. Andreas pulled out the gun and aimed it at him. A shot came from his mouth. He pointed the gun at each of his brothers and me and made an enormous number of firing sounds. A veritable hailstorm of shots came from his mouth. Joseph's expression didn't change. Martin kept sleeping. Petrus shouted: Enough! That's when I got scared.

◆

When it was summer once again, the summer holidays just begun, I knocked at Petrus's door at the end of a seemingly endless work-day at the Department of Transportation cafeteria and asked if he knew where the catalogue for the Giacometti exhibition that I'd bought the day before was. He shook his head, looked up briefly from his desk and said: I'm going to visit Joseph in Canada.

It only occurred to you just now?

Just now?

Petrus always repeated part of any question he was not willing to answer. And, as always, it made me furious.

Did you decide this a while ago?

A while ago? No.

Did you book your flight?

My flight? Of course.

And when is your flight?

When? On Monday.

What, Monday already? In three days?

Four.

And where is the goddamn Giacometti catalogue?

Giacometti? In the bathroom, sorry, I—

Thanks. I slammed the door.

I was jealous. Of Joseph. Of all the people Petrus would meet in Canada, of every tree and bear in Canada, what a stupid word when you said it slowly, one syllable at a time, Ca-na-da, why hadn't I noticed it before. What a stupid country. What a stupid brother. Joseph, that bristle-bearded forest-dweller. Have a lot of fun and stimulating conversations with that mute, autistic voyeur! Petrus didn't even ask me. Sure, I had to work and, sure, I didn't have any money, but he didn't even ask me! Had he asked someone else? His secret lover? I thought of the letter, the longish envelope he had quickly slipped into his pocket when he noticed I was watching him at the mailbox in France a year earlier. Again and again I'd wondered what was with the letter. If he had a lover. And she was going to fly with him to Canada? Nonsense. But why not me? Why hadn't he even asked me? And why, why couldn't he release me, *without being asked,* from my horrible poverty and simply hand me a plane ticket with a kiss on the forehead? I couldn't stand this cafeteria one more day, not one single day. And I couldn't stand the medical officer who stopped in five times a day *for a quick chat* and bought yet another diet cola, another chocolate bar, either. Out of the question that I should have to put up for one more day with the smell of the daily special or of the dishwashing station where bleach seemed to couple with vomit. I just couldn't take one more day of listening to the well-intentioned encouragement of my co-worker who'd been on the job for years, not to mention the summer hits on the radio when she would turn up the volume with a smile and a wink before and after the lunch hour.

And yet, every morning I took the number thirteen streetcar all the way across town to the Department of Transportation, twenty-three stations I could rattle off backward and forward in as aloof and neutral a tone as the woman's voice on the recording. Next stop: Tunnelstrasse. I took on her slack voice and tonelessly listed everything I saw. Next glimpse: traveling salesman in a hurry. Next glimpse: tired drunk, dozing off. Next glimpse: exhausted worker, shivering. I stuck to the voice all day long, internally and externally, using it for my internal monologues and for interactions with the customers. Next glimpse: head of a family in an ill-fitting suit—soup of the day: bouillon with egg, yes, of course, we can leave out the parsley. Next glimpse: pancake makeup in a hideous shade of beige on office worker's face—we're out of sweetener, unfortunately, it will be delivered tomorrow. Next glimpse: exasperating medical officer, where's the hammer—you again, Doctor, that was quick, another diet cola? A little chocolate? Both?

Hey you, don't start with me—he was always very familiar—don't even start! That damn sweetener. I guzzle the cola and I get really hungry. So I devour the chocolate. Then I have a guilty conscious and a raging thirst on top of it all. So then I drink another cola and get even more hungry. It's horrible. Just don't start with me. You see what artificial sweetener leads to in pig farming: piglets eat beyond their hunger, way beyond, they get fatter and fatter! Look at me!

My automatic station-stop voice forbade me from answering: Then go ahead and drink a real soda with real sugar, Doctor, that should solve your problem according to your logic. No, the voice said: it's not easy for you either, Doctor, is it? One cola, one chocolate bar, that'll be three francs forty, as always. Enjoy.

How long will you be away?
How long?
Yes, when are you coming back from Canada?
Back? In about three weeks, more or less.
So, end of July?

End of July? More like early August, I think.

Oh, kiss my ass. No, I didn't actually say that. I probably said something like: Good, now I know for sure. Have a good trip.

One evening Andreas was standing at my door. Sitting at my door. The neighbor wanted to call the police, he said. His scar moved when he talked. It looked fresh and had a blue sheen. I tried to remember his mouth before he was bitten. His beautiful, soft mouth. The gentle curve of his lips, which were so sanguine, they almost looked like he was wearing lipstick. What? he asked. Nothing, I said and unlocked the door. I let him in and made coffee. For several days, it had hurt whenever I swallowed. Now it didn't. I looked at him. From the side his eyes just looked dark, they were so deep-set. Andreas? He turned his head. Yes? They were blue. You want sugar? Yes, no, oh—he smiled at me, his scar stuck out—I don't actually drink coffee. Now they were gray, his eyes, definitely.

He invited me out to dinner. He had heard of an interesting spot nearby, he said. What brought you here? I asked. He laughed, his scar swelled. I was startled, for a second it had looked like a tiny, twitching amphibian, a primeval mini-ichthyostega. He waved the waiter over and when they couldn't agree after several minutes, the manager came to our table, shook Andreas's hand, shook mine. My sister-in-law, Andreas introduced me, I nodded and gave a faint smile. The manager invited him down to the wine cellar. I sat at the table alone for a while.

Your lips are all blue, Andreas said, would you like a coffee with dessert?

I wiped my mouth with my napkin. No thank you, I said, or I won't sleep.

Still blue. Are you tired?

Yes, and I have to get up early. Better?

No.

I stood up and went to the ladies' room, rinsed out my mouth, moistened my lips and scraped the crust of red wine from the corners of my mouth. I looked up, saw my face in the mirror and felt ashamed. But I'm not doing anything, I murmured and went back into the dining room.

Do you need anything else, a hand towel?

A toothbrush wouldn't be bad.

Sorry, I've only got mine. I threw him a hand towel and said: I'm going to bed.

Lie down, he said and grinned.

I'd been waiting for that phrase all evening. He hadn't said it and that won me over to such an extent that I was thinking maybe he wasn't such a bad person after all. And now this. If you need anything, let me know. Otherwise, good night, I said in an unfriendly tone.

Good night, he said, giving me a look. Now his eyes were green.

I closed my door, opened the window, and lay down. My bed was big. Sometimes at night Petrus came to my room, but mostly in the morning. Rarely did we go to bed together in the evening. What could he be doing now, in the wilds of Canada? How late was it there? Just before six PM, he had the whole evening ahead of him. Well, Petrus, make good use of it, I said, and for later, when you go to sleep: sweet dreams. Good night.

I lay there and smiled into the darkness.

I kissed the scar, I worked over its bulges and hollows with my tongue and lips as if I wanted to suck the last bit of life out of it. Your mouth, you had such a beautiful mouth, I said. Yes, that one was stolen, he said. Kissed away from an angel. No: I wheedled it off him, now he's got mine. But this mouth here, with this peculiar lip, I'm not giving it up. I'm not trading it for anyone's.

In retrospect, I described him as an incubus who descended on me without my wanting him to, but that's not how it was. I dreamed about him, that's true, dreamed he was moving on top of and inside me and in my dream I wondered when the neighbors would finally call the police because the cries that escaped me could surely be heard all the way to Canada, and I said, Watch out, the cops are about to show up. Andreas wanted to roll off me and I woke up.

I stood in Petrus's door.

I said: Are you coming?

And Andreas said: Yes.

The next morning Andreas was agitated, he seemed both absent and harried. I have to call him, he said when I asked him if he wanted breakfast. He dialed Joseph's number in Canada and woke them both from a sound sleep. They could barely speak. Joseph handed Petrus the receiver and Petrus kept asking: What's the matter? Did something happen? It's the middle of the night! And Andreas exclaimed: Guess where I am! Yes, of course she's here. You know how she is, not exactly charming, but she didn't leave her brother-in-law out in the rain. But for real, your bed, it's terrible, much too soft. I didn't get a wink of—

Petrus hung up. Andreas was pale. He looked at me: He knows.

But Petrus didn't know anything.

I found the letter only much later. It was in the Bible. The perfect hiding place, actually. Why I took the Bible off the shelf and opened it, I no longer remember, but the letter fell right into my hands and before I checked the date, I knew from the French address that it was the letter I had looked for in vain in Petrus's room the night Andreas was bitten. It was from a certain Miriam, but the contents were so harmless that I didn't understand what it was doing in this remote place. The contrast between the innocuous contents and the ingenious hiding place made the whole thing suspicious. I knew it, I said to myself, but I didn't know anything.

I just googled Miriam's name. She's alive, a million-fold. And since I don't know her last name, how alive she is won't change. My dog presses up against me. She whimpers and fidgets, she wants to go out. She sat under my desk and let me write long enough. Who would have thought, would have thought at the time, that I'd have a dog like this, that is half like this, she's only a border collie mix. She still loves sheep, though, but she's not nearly as well-trained as the Lie-downs and doesn't speak any English as far as I know.

3

Twelve autumns

At first, winter did not want to come, now it won't go. Mid-February and it's snowing, snowing, snowing.

My husband walked the dog and took the children to kindergarten. On a sled, believe it or not. The sidewalks are cross-country skiing trails, he says when he comes home for a nap, before his afternoon shift begins.

The dog shakes herself.

My husband gives me a long kiss, it tastes good. Just as I'm noticing this, he flinches, looks at his mobile phone and says: Just a second, I'll only be a second—and disappears around the corner into his room.

After about a minute, he comes back.

What's going on? I ask.

Everything's fine.

What was so urgent?

Don't worry about it, everything's fine.

I'm not worried!

Yes, you are and you don't need to be. Stop catastrophizing, it doesn't suit you, he says and kisses me again, and even though I'm not in the mood, this short kiss tastes very good, too. I'm going to lie down, he says. His door closes.

I sit at my desk, open a new document and stare at the blank screen. And now? In the beginning was Petrus, it all started with him. He led me to Andreas. The story could end here.

Just as I finish writing this, an enormous shadow comes up behind me, sways closer, grows larger, covers my screen in darkness. Petrus? I turn around. My husband is standing behind me. Who are you talking to? he asks. I thought you were going to take a nap, I reply. What are you doing? he asks. Working, I say and, since he's looking at me skeptically, I add: writing.

Who are you writing? he asks.

Who? What do you mean? I'm writing a book, maybe you remember. Here, chapter three, slow going. At this rate, I'll still be sitting here in ten years.

My husband turns to leave. Don't worry, everything's fine, I say. He stops. That's my line, he says. We both smile, briefly, then he shakes his head and leaves.

No, the story can't end here. I look out at the driving snow. It's ten in the morning and still not really light out. You'd think it was late afternoon. Petrus. The last thing he saw was more or less what I see now: twilight, heavy snow. He left, unnoticed and without saying goodbye. Suddenly he's here again, but at the same time I miss him. He lays his heavy, warm hand on the back of my neck, encircles it, presses gently at first, then harder and harder, pushing me forward. Petrus, then Andreas: the beginning of a series, if you're going to take the names seriously, a series of twelve, twelve names, twelve men, one after the other.

How many loves does anyone have? If I kept on with my story, would I end up with twelve? Probably not. And yet: the way I count depends on what I tell. But one thing is certain: however I count, whatever I tell, my husband should come last. *No man after my husband. Period.* I write on a piece of scrap paper, which I don't pin up on the wall as usual, but slip under my keyboard.

Twelve . . . I think it over and make a rough guess. If I stay on track and continue chronologically, then my husband will be number five. But maybe I'll find a solution on the way, as I write? Perhaps enter higher spheres of love, free of corporeality, in Plato's pure realm? (Personally, I don't believe it for a minute.) Or in the innocent higher elevations of imagination? I pull the note out from under my keyboard and tear it up.

The knocking again, the hammering overhead. I don't know what I'm hatching. I've had a cold for weeks now. But not more than that—except for the knocking in my head! In the meantime, I've gotten a handle on the Morse code. But the better I know it, the less clear the messages become. All I can recognize is * * * / - - / - - - / - * - / * : SMOKE. Before and after, a wild, nonsensical chaos of dots and dashes. There are moments when TIME or KID are also hammered out, but today, at best, there's SMOKE. Why that should remind me of my dog, who will be ten years old in a few days, I don't know. I make a note that I need to get her a birthday present and go back to chapter three. The knocking has to stop, it must stop! So then. One after the other. Man for man. After Petrus and Andreas would come Jakob. Yes, that fits.

When the leaves fall, it's time for his birthday, he said. He knew this even when he was little and it's still true today, unlike the other childhood pillars of truth that have collapsed. The one about eternity, for example, and the one about our benevolent God the father, the one about justice, and above all, the one about love. But on this one, he can rely: in autumn the leaves always fell and he always turned a year older.

As soon as the clocks are changed, everything goes very quickly, he said. With the darkness, the leaves fell, as did the rain, sometimes even the first snow, he had his birthday and something happened. *Something always happened.*

The autumn we fell in love was a golden one. Even if Jakob later claimed it was as dark and rainy as every other autumn. The days were sunny well into November, the nights were clear and cold. During the day, the foliage glowed an intense yellow and at night, huge spider webs shimmered in the light of the lanterns on the boardwalk. We sat on a bench and listened. After a while we could hear the spiders at work. We could distinguish their fine weaving from the rushing of the river, which was especially loud because of a marked drop in elevation. We looked at each other and said: I can hear it. And said: So can I. And we kissed each other very quietly.

It ends the way it begins, my grandmother always said. She probably didn't mean relationships, because for her they weren't finite. Even though she longed for the end as she had never longed for anyone or anything in her life before. The end meant: his end, Grandfather's death. When it finally came, she suddenly looked relieved and much younger, almost girlish. She enjoyed the attention she got and smiled coquettishly. She received condolences like compliments and answered them by shyly batting her eyelashes. Not much later, she died, too. It ends the way it begins. This sentence often comes back to me.

Things began covertly with Jakob and me. As a game with our feet, a lively conversation between his left and my right foot during a theater performance.

Petrus and I were still a couple even though we hadn't been living together for about a year; I had left Zurich and the university and applied to the Salzburg Drama School to study acting and directing. Petrus was against it, though he did end up following me halfway. He enrolled for one unhappy semester in Vienna and another in Munich. He spent weekends with me, but mostly without me. On days off, I'd get a key from the doorman and rehearse one of my directing projects with grateful acting students who hated quiet weekends. Minna von Barnhelm's dialogue with Tellheim, for example.

Will you answer one question?
Any, Madam.
With nothing more than a simple yes or no?
I will—if I can.
Do you still love me, Tellheim?
Madam, this question—
You must know what is happening in your heart. Do you still love

me, Tellheim—Yes or no?
  If my heart—
  Yes or no!
  Then, yes!
  Yes?
  Yes, yes!—and yet—

What does he mean, *and yet*? the actor playing Tellheim asked and the actress playing Minna took a step back and rolled her eyes. I'm sorry, but I don't get it, he insisted, my demeanor in this passage, I mean Tellheim's demeanor. So, is he saying clearly yes or rather yes and no?

Yes, Petrus and I were a couple even after my friend Katrin told me a secret one day under the dripping awning of an ice cream store, a secret she *absolutely* couldn't keep to herself any longer: Petrus had betrayed me with her. Or she me with Petrus, you could also look at it that way. Doubly betrayed by lover and friend, that's how to put it. It happened a year before, no, even more, but that's not important, she said. She believed there was no statute of limitations for something like this. None. I tried to follow her logic, I plunged the long spoon deep into the glass and scooped a chunk of chocolate ice cream up from the bottom, pulled the spoon out slowly, balanced it in my mouth, pushed it in and was surprised that it was empty. I looked at my lap, at the ugly brown spot on my light-colored trousers. That's disgusting, I said and grabbed a napkin, but all I did was rub the stain deeper into the fabric. Later, I went to rehearsal. While I watched my three actresses improvising, I thought of one applicant who a few weeks before had shown up at auditions with a monologue from *Faust* and had been accepted with enthusiasm; a huge talent, the leader of the audition committee had said, and once he learns how to work, he'll be a candidate for the A list. He has star potential, no doubt about it. I thought he was cute. Actually there were two cute ones, but the one with star potential had looked over at me several times, when I was called into the auditions as student representative, and now I remembered him. His name was either Jakob Bäumer or Jonas Liebig. Those were the names of the two cute ones on the list of accepted students.

Let's call it a day and go get a drink, I said, and the actresses were surprised that we were stopping when it was still light out.

We were working on my first production. It was during semester break. In the morning I worked in a bakery, so we could start rehearsals at three in the afternoon. I had chosen, no surprise, Samuel Beckett's *Come and Go*. Three women sit on a bench. In turn, one rises and leaves briefly, upon which the other two whisper a secret to each other about the third. The secrets themselves are not revealed. Nor are we told where each went and what she did while she was gone. What bound the three? Why did each return? What's fascinating is what is not heard and not said—and, of course, what isn't seen. This play (the word is misleading, it's a short play, at best a "dramaticule," as Beckett called it) is less than five minutes long, if you follow his meticulous stage directions. I let the actresses improvise for hours and they developed endless dialogues and back-stories I had them write out at home only to cross out everything shortly before the premiere. Not a single word was spoken that did not come from Beckett, and yet the running time was at least two hours. At least, that is, because the doors were opened after two hours. The play continued until there was no one left in the audience. Over and over again, from the beginning.

At the premiere, at the start of the new semester in early October, I sat in the middle of the first row, Petrus to my left, Jakob to my right. It was only Jakob's second day, but he still rushed energetically through the auditorium right up to the stage. He had seen me and sat down next to me without hesitating. Good evening.

Hello. I looked at him severely.

Good luck!

You're supposed to say break a leg.

Are you?

Yes.

Well then, break a leg! He became engrossed in the program notes.

When the auditorium lights went down, his foot nudged mine for the first time. When the dramaticule was on its third round, he knocked again. By the fifth round our feet had started up a timid conversation and by the eighth they were engaged in a lively discussion. At the same time I was holding Petrus's damp hand in my left, squeezing it tenderly. I glanced at him from time to time. Jakob, by contrast, I did not look at once.

It took forever for everyone in the audience to leave. The actresses were relieved when it was finally over, but they were also disappointed since there was no one left to applaud, except for Petrus, Jakob, and me. One of the three was so exhausted, she wept. You were fantastic, I said, thank you so much. Petrus and Jakob nodded. Petrus did not speak for an hour, then he said: Three is always one too many.

What do you mean?

Well, people are always forming pairs. Whenever someone stands up, the other two scoot closer together.

I nodded. He nodded back and explained why my staging didn't hold.

The minimum a theatrical production must do is to tell a story, it can be a very short one, however banal or simple it may be, right? When, like tonight, there's no beginning or end, then it's not a story.

The story is precisely that it never ends, I reply.

Petrus considers this briefly. The play isn't called *Go and Come*, but *Come and Go*. At the end, you go. At the end you can just leave.

You think?

I do.

Jakob thought I was great. I was a year older, one year ahead of him, and I was a director. He wanted to be seen by me, and for me to direct him. He wanted me to tell him how talented he was, which, in fact, he was. With you as my director, I could play any role, he said, any at all and in every one, I'd be good, really good. I did perception exercises with him. I blindfolded him and put him in the middle of a rehearsal room. I moved silently across the floor toward him and then away. The task was simple: when he thought I was within reach, he had to stretch his arm out in my direction. At first, every attempt, with an impatient click of his tongue, went astray. No commenting, I admonished him. You determine reality. You feel it out and make it visible. Understood? And at some point, I stood at the other end of the room and he extended his hand toward me and smiled instead of clicking his tongue, and I saw his hand start to stroke the air. Very good, I called out, keep going. Gradually a woman's entire body began to take shape under his caressing hands. You're making me jealous, I said, and I came up to him from behind and took off his blindfold. He turned around, and we were all over each other. That's how almost every perception exercise ended. Afterward we lay exhausted in each other's arms and discussed the exercise. You get better every day, I said, and he bit my shoulder from joy.

At first I didn't notice his sadness. My grandmother always said: There's no reason to be sad, sweetheart. She would say this in such a sorrowful tone that I would be overcome with sadness. I knew a thing or two about unhappiness, but I didn't see it in Jakob until autumn came again. Mornings, he overslept. At noon, he just watched others eat. At night, he couldn't fall asleep. I'm going to go out for a beer, he'd say. Late at night, he would sit at the kitchen table, as if lying in wait for something. We were going to celebrate his birthday. I don't like birthdays, he said, but I had already organized everything. When he was with the other acting students, he perked up. He made fun of some new couples who couldn't keep their hands off each other. Everyone was always switching

partners, only the two of us stayed together. We were *the couple.*
Jakob announced: People, if you really intend to get it on with
everyone once, then hurry up, get down to business and on to the
next! When I whistle, rotate, understood? One dream couple is
enough, someone shouted back, not everyone can have a steady
love life like you, Jakob. When are you two getting married, actually? Jakob and I looked at each other and smiled. And without
having agreed on it, we both started to improvise on the theme
We're expecting a child. Our performance was discreet, spreading
the news only by the way we touched, the way we smiled at each
other and shared our secret. We constructed the game slowly,
over half the evening, and when we were finally dancing, holding
each other close, and he caressed me very tenderly, everyone suddenly saw. That I drank enormous amounts of alcohol didn't seem
to bother anyone, the news hit like a bombshell. A few asked: Are
you happy? Others squealed: Oh, how cute. They all gave me hugs
and patted Jakob on the back. What talented actors we were. We
were so turned on, we were all over each other all night long and
didn't get any sleep.

Jakob's mother called the following morning. His father was
in intensive care. A stroke. Jakob dropped his head into his hands
and nodded.

12 x autumn could be an equation for our relationship because
it's true that something always happened in the fall. In our third
autumn I realized that I really was pregnant. Actually, Jakob realized it. He bought a kit and made me do the urine test. For days
I'd felt dizzy and had headaches. I went straight back to bed while
Jakob hung the test strip in the cup. Look at this, he said, oh shit.
He held the damp strip under my nose.

Leave me alone.

Look at it!

I couldn't see anything. But the headache wouldn't go away.
I went to the doctor a week later. Look at this, he also said and

pointed at the screen of the ultrasound machine, there's a little heart beating quite clearly. I couldn't see anything there either. But I made an appointment in a private clinic in Vienna. We split the cost. I respect whatever choice you make, Jakob had said, but for me, at this point, it's unthinkable, completely beyond the realm of the possible. It was an outpatient procedure with local anesthetic. Jakob held my hand and sang in my ear because the noises from the suction were too horrible for him to bear. He sang a few Brecht songs, each dodgier than the last, until I asked him to stop and go outside. We were staying on the Donau canal with an acquaintance of our acting teacher. She said: Damn, yes, I know the clinic, I've been there three, no, four times.

The doctor had told me I should lie down, for a few days if possible. Two days after, it was Jakob's birthday. We went to the Prater. I rode on the Ferris wheel, went through the tunnel of horror, ate cotton candy, and threw up.

Love is not something you choose, dear heart, my grandmother always said and stroked my cheek. Even today, when I hear the word *heart,* I touch my cheek, my left cheek. Afterward I got pimples, no that's not it exactly, I broke out all over my neck, chest, and stomach, everywhere and for months. My skin was bright red and as bumpy as a turkey in breeding season, and it itched so badly that I scratched myself bloody. I became stricter. You just have to work harder, Jakob, I said, a lot of people have talent. I cast him in my next production, Genet's *The Maids.* As the playwright recommends, I had men play the two maids. Jakob was one, Jonas Liebig the other. I still have to think about who should play Madame, who is off-stage the entire first part, I said. But it was clear to everyone that I was the one for the part. Once, after I criticized Jakob too harshly in rehearsal, Jonas wanted out of the show. I'm sorry, but this is horrible, no one wants to have to watch, he said. So I became gentler. I could only humiliate Jakob to a degree Jonas could stand. As a result, from my point of view, I was working against the material and against the play, which, finally—and exclusively—was about power games and debasement in all conceivable variations, beyond all mercy. Naturally, it all escalated the moment Madame walked on stage. I stood there and gave the two men commands on all levels, as employer, as director, and as a woman, and Jonas Liebig was not the only one for whom it was too much. Jakob tore off his apron. The project fell apart, but our relationship was saved.

One autumn later, I'd finished my studies and begun my first theater job in Zurich. From that point on and for the rest of our time together, we led a long-distance relationship. Jakob bought a car. When he drove me, my mattress, a few books, and a trunk of my clothes to Zurich in his green, 1980 Ford, he said he was happy. Then he looked through the windshield at the sky. Autumn's coming, he said. Look where you're going, I yelled. Jakob yanked the steering wheel around.

We bought our first mobile phones. The first call Jakob received was from me. I stood next to him and asked if he could hear me. The second was from his mother. His father had had another stroke. A *semi-serious* one this time, but his father wouldn't be able to come home. Jakob cried until his battery was dead and the connection lost.

Jakob's father recovered before Christmas and was able to celebrate Christmas Eve at home. In spring they hired him a Czech nurse, who claimed he tried to be intimate with her. When Jakob heard about it, he became exuberant with relief and asked me if I'd like "get intimate with him, intimate like the Czechs," and this was our code, which we eventually shortened to *get Czech*. Jakob had gotten an offer from the Salzburg Landestheater in spring, but he turned it down contemptuously. He couldn't stand the blinkered, narrow-minded, hostile provincial city for two more years, he announced, that hick theater can stage its ham-fisted burlesques without him in the future.

It was autumn again. Jakob drove from theater to theater and auditioned, but against all predictions and bets made in the theater academy, he was not overwhelmed with offers. In fact, he was turned down over and over again. His father died at the end of November. I don't get it, Jakob said, I just don't get it. He looked at me, seeking my help. Something's finally got to work out, he said. In the end, it was almost Christmas when he signed up with the Salzburg Landestheater. I moved to Frankfurt, which didn't bring us any closer. When we weren't working, we were commuting. He by car, me by train. When I didn't have any weekend rehearsals or performances, I took the night train, drank a bottle of red wine in the dining car, and collapsed onto the bunk. In the morning, my head was pounding. I got out in the Upper Austrian no-man's land, changed to the regional express, and craved a coffee. I was sure I would die if the man with the cart—who never came—didn't pass by right away. Or Jakob would get in his car right after rehearsals, sometimes even after performances, and drive to my place. He drove until he arrived, in one go. It took a few hours before his legs and tongue could move easily again. By then I had usually fallen asleep.

If you're tired, go to sleep, my grandmother always said. Sleep heals, Goethe even said this, though I couldn't find it anywhere when I systematically combed through the fourteen volumes of Goethe's collected works. I had planned on working the adage about sleep into my eulogy. The family had decided unanimously, although with a few abstentions, that I should deliver the eulogy at my grandmother's graveside, me, the favorite grandchild, me, who *had been trained in this kind of thing, after all.* I was too sad to write and Goethe, again, was no help. So I had no choice but to tell the mourners what Grandmother would have said in this situation: there's no reason to be sad, sweetheart, everything ends the way it begins and if you're tired, go to sleep. At this, everyone started crying and said I had put it so well.

Jakob, who always had trouble falling asleep in autumn, wasn't able to stay awake one November night somewhere between Nürnberg and Würzberg. It was our sixth autumn. He was at the wheel of his old Escort, driving to my place for the hundredth time. I calculated that it must have been about the one-hundred-and-forty-fourth time. He had often described the accidents he'd seen on the way, scenes of accidents he passed. Again and again, when I sat next to him in the car, we'd driven by the misfortunes of others. At Christmas time once, when the road ahead of us suddenly turned white, I called out:

Snow!

Snow?

Snow!

A Hungarian truck had crashed into the guardrail and overturned. Most of its load was strewn over the road. The cars following it had run over the packages and crushed them. What I took for snow was laundry detergent. I don't know which alarmed us more: the colorful shreds of plastic flung against the windshield or the sight of the lifeless body two firemen were pulling out of the driver's cab. We saw similar sights in every season on expressways, rural highways, and avenues: demolished or burning sports cars, motorcycles, and minivans. We saw severely injured men, women, and children. In every season except the fall. It could be there were fewer accidents in autumn; it could be that we were too preoccupied with our own unhappiness to notice them. This time it was Jakob in his Escort who lost control and flipped over. Afterward, he was completely alert. He couldn't move. He called me. I was the director, I should tell him what to do.

Where are you?

In the middle of the road.

Have you called the police?

No.

Start the car.

Doesn't work.

Do you know your location?

No. Yes, wait, no, No, I don't

What do you see around you?

Nothing.

I called the police. In the light of dawn, they delivered him to my door. Somehow he had managed to get to the shoulder. That saved his life, one of the officers explained, take good care of him. Jakob sat there absently. I've been thinking things over, he said when they left, you need to work on new roles with me. I can't stand this two-bit company any longer. I'm the one who determines reality, remember? I'm the one! Me!

So it all started again. I directed him. I challenged him. I harried him. I treated him like a child, the child I didn't have. My first demand was that he find suitable roles himself, my second was that, from now on, as soon as he got behind the wheel, he start talking. I told him he had to name every single thing he saw while driving, absolutely everything. He had to read aloud every sign he laid eyes on. That was the only way, I said with complete conviction, to avoid the danger of nodding off. It took Jakob an effort to get over his self-consciousness, especially when I was sitting next to him. He said he felt like an idiot, but he got used to it after a few months.

He couldn't find any roles he liked, so after making a few derisive comments, I looked for some. Shakespeare, Kleist, Büchner, I said, Malvolio, Achilles, Woyzeck: hit, hit, miss. It would be ridiculous if we couldn't land you a first-class offer with these. Jakob hugged me. I was determined to get the best, or at least the best possible from him. I was not squeamish in choosing my means. When we rehearsed Woyzeck, I'd watch him for a while, then shout at him as if I weren't the director, but an opponent in the play, the doctor experimenting with him as with a lab rat. I've seen Woyzeck; he pissed on the street, pissed against a wall, like a dog. When we rehearsed Malvolio, I immediately treated him like the character. I addressed him as *Jakob* and asked how he could seriously think his mistress had written him a love letter. When we rehearsed Achilles, I was merciless: Excuse me, but your love, not convincing, I don't buy it. And he tried again and again, he pleaded, he ranted, he raved, he roared, and when he finally lost hope, I said: very good so far, OK, tomorrow we'll do more.

In the spring, he suddenly announced he had fallen in love. He told me he'd overestimated me, my instincts weren't great or I'd have noticed signs long ago. I couldn't tell if I felt shocked or relieved. I felt weightless. It has to stop, I said. He left. The following weekend, he was back. It's over, he said.

This or that?

That. He raised his chin and gestured vaguely into the distance. Before he drove off, he said: the entire time, I was dying to tell you how great I felt. To talk about how wonderful it is to be in love. To share the feeling with you. Can you understand that?

No.

I love you. He gave me a kiss and got in his new car, a used VW Passat. He rolled down the window. There's too much distance between us, he said. We both nodded. Safe drive! I waved as he drove away. He turned at the corner and I saw that his lips were moving, as always. *One-way street. Two-way bicycle traffic. Speed limit thirty.* And as always, I found it both touching and embarrassing.

I looked for a job near him. The theater in Graz was hiring under new management. I'd heard that Graz was a beautiful city, a little off the beaten path in a far southeastern corner of the German-speaking world, why on earth would I want to go there, but it was beautiful, I'd been told. As soon as I signed the contract in Graz, he revealed he had just quit in Salzburg and was moving to Berlin, where he wanted to give it a try as a *freelance.* Somehow, I have the feeling we're always missing each other, I said.

When autumn came and his birthday was approaching, he showed up twice unannounced and rang the doorbell, even though he had a key, and asked me if I was alone.

He became clingy. He visited me much more often than before. The nine hundred kilometers didn't bother him, he said, not at all, eight hours, what's the problem? He could spend his time how he liked, now that he was freelance. He might just as well have said unemployed. He spent his days on the expressway and nights, the vast majority of them, in my bed. He ran out of money, stayed for weeks at a time, cooked for me, went grocery shopping, managed the household. He was interested only in current political events. He skipped through the news channels around the clock. The world was unbearable, he said, and the new millennium hasn't changed a thing, on the contrary, I should take a look at all the injustice, it was beyond all measure, enough to make you crazy. He turned off the television. He told me he had a few meetings in Berlin early in the new year. He was preparing his film career. His visits gradually tapered off and when spring arrived, he asked me one evening to come as soon as possible. I called in sick, missed the night train, and took the earliest train, changing three times. He picked me up at the station and told me he had fallen in love. I replied that first I needed some sleep, would that be possible?

I lay on his mattress and thought of the phrase I hadn't said at my grandmother's funeral, the only one I didn't drop into her grave. It stuck to me like polyester resin or gecko feet on a sheer rock face. I just couldn't get rid of it: Love is not something you choose, dear heart. She stroked my cheek. I smiled at her and said: this has to stop.

The knocking has stopped. It's quiet. But my eyes are burning. I see the many black letters on the screen before me, dancing up and down. I touch my cheek. Oh, Grandmother. What exactly is love? How can it come and go? Where does it go, when it's gone?

4

A stranger I will leave

I have a fever. My neck hurts and my ears are ringing. At first I thought it was just the Morse Code in my skull—which I've almost gotten used to—always hammering out the same words in dots and dashes: Smoke. Time. Child. But for a few days now, it hurts whenever I move and I'm barely able to walk the dog and pick the children up from kindergarten, to play with them, pamper them, cook for them, take care of them, and crawl into bed. My husband has the late shift almost every day. During the day, while I'm working, when I'm in my office writing, he lies in bed or watches television. He can't seem to get any rest and is permanently exhausted; very rarely there's an invisible flash inside him. He perks up and types wildly on his laptop keyboard before sinking back onto his pillow and jabbing at the remote with his thumbs.

Come on, keep going! One after the other, I murmur as I make myself a cup of coffee in the kitchen, one leads to the next, one love into the next. Or does love always stay the same, always true to itself? Is it only the vessels that change? Does love simply present itself in one man after another, does it reveal itself as the one and only true love, just in several guises? Does love not have several faces then, but only the beloved's? One after the other, man for man . . . Johannes . . . I think back as I fill the water tank of the coffee machine, yes, there was a Johannes.

Did you say something? My husband is standing behind me.

No, I was talking to the dog. That we'd go out later. My husband looks at me, watches me put the pod in the machine.

Tea would be better for you, he says.

I nod, put my cup on the tray and push the button.

You look unwell, he says.

So do you, I reply.

He gives me a concerned look. I'll get the thermometer.

That instrument is a weapon. You press it against someone's forehead and press the button. A blue laser beam shoots out. After a few seconds, it beeps and a number appears on the display. 103 degrees. The warning light blinks.

One hundred and three? Crazy!

Give it to me, I say, and turn the laser on him. 99.3. No blinking.

Go lie down, he says.

I have to get back to my desk, I'm right in the middle of my story, I reply.

No, you have to go to bed, my husband says. He takes me by the hand and leads me to bed. Sleep, he says. Somehow, he seems sad.

The pillow feels like cement. Although I sink into it, it's as hard as stone. When I close my eyes I see a dark tunnel. Two round headlights shine in my eyes. I turn my head to the other side and suddenly there's a train coming from that direction, too. What's going on here? I recognize the sight. I'm in Berlin and twelve years younger. I've just been left. I'm in my own story. My head is pounding. Could you bring me an aspirin? I want to call out, but realize I don't even know my husband yet.

The subways are coming from the right and the left. Both trains look like giant toys, bright yellow and lightweight. *Ruhleben* it says on the train heading out of the city. Ruhleben, peaceful living, that sounds good, I knock on the corrugated aluminum and board. After ten minutes the train reaches the final stop. I stay in my seat. The power is turned off, a brief humming noise, silence. I go to the door. It won't open. I sit back down. A man on the platform looks at me and signals at me to get out of the car. I turn my head away and stare at the gravel on the adjacent track, then at my hands, then at the sky.

I have a plane ticket in my bag, a little money, and my key ring. I left my telephone on Jakob's kitchen table. I must have lost consciousness in my sleep, fifteen hours, it is possible I slept that long. It was three in the afternoon when I woke up with an aching, burning head. Jakob was gone. I even checked the pantry. He was gone. I called him and flinched. His cell phone rang shrilly on the kitchen table. I put mine next to it.

I left his apartment. There was a travel agency catty-corner across the street. I crossed the four-lane avenue on a diagonal. A taxi honked, a roller-blader yelled: Hey, be sure you make it to shore. The woman in the travel agency was on the phone. She was whispering. I waited. From time to time I gave her a look, she gestured with her hand, then covered her mouth and the receiver. I wouldn't have understood anything anyway. In the middle of the week, at short notice, and one way: expensive, she said once she'd finished her conversation. Sandra Bolle-Reichelt was written on the sign at her desk. Are you married? I asked as she typed on her keyboard with incredible speed. Why? she asked in return. Because of your name. I was wondering if you used to be called Reichelt or Bolle and why you didn't just go with Reichelt and above all why you didn't drop the Bolle. No—I only thought that part. All I said was: Because of your name. I inherited it, she said.

Aha, I replied, although I didn't understand.

Should we get back to your booking? I nodded. She pointed out that *as a rule* a train ticket is cheaper, but I explained that I had to go as quickly as possible and as soon as possible. I can't spend another sixteen hours sitting in a train, there was no way, I'd only arrived the day before. Up to you, she said. Thank you. I booked a flight to Vienna. I would decide there how I'd continue.

And what if he calls me now? If he tries, again and again, to reach me? At some point it will occur to him to check his apartment, it's not impossible that I might have died of sorrow. Hopefully he's already on his way, right this minute, and hopefully he's scared of what he'll find. And then? He'll find our two cell phones next to each other on the table, nothing more.

After a brief thrumming, there's a jolt. The subway starts moving again. Now I'm facing away from the direction of travel. The hands on the station clock are pointing straight up and down. Sixteen more hours until my flight leaves. A clear evening. After ten minutes, I stand up without thinking and go to the door, but when the train stops, I don't push the button. I sit back down. If I had my phone, I could call Regine. I haven't seen her for a long time. I count the stations passing. Sixteen. I easily find the way to the pub she once showed me, Regine, my friend from university. My living room, she called it, I suddenly remember as I open the door. I look around but she's not there.

When he walks in, he looks me directly in the eye. Piercing light blue eyes that seem familiar. He sits at the bar. I think about his eyes and where I could have seen them before. I draw the shape of his eyes on the beer coaster, almond-shaped and slightly slanted and when he turns and gives me another look, I know: they're dog eyes, the eyes of a Siberian husky. I stipple countless dots on the beer coaster, little pricks, actually. I finally stop and recognize the shape of a five o'clock shadow under the husky eyes, just like his.

When I pay, he slides off the barstool, bends down and ties his shoelaces. I stand right in front of him. I look at his part. He briefly raises his head and looks at me with his husky eyes. Then he ties the laces of his other shoe.

I wait for him outside. He comes out after only a few seconds. It looks to me like he nods slightly. I turn away and start walking.

Evening is falling. I walk into the twilight, it envelops me, and with every step I enter more deeply into the darkness. My footsteps are soundless in the traffic noise. Between the car lanes, in the middle of the road, a tramcar screeches around the curve and comes toward me. Left and right, two lanes of cars pass by. At the first opportunity, I'll turn onto a quiet side street. The first opportunity takes a while to come. I suppress the urge to turn around, and pick up my pace.

As soon as I'm on the side street, I hear a bird singing. I stop and listen. It sounds like it's carrying the heavy weight of disappointed love, long and fluted, melodious and piquant, touching and insistent at the same time, but mostly very, very loud. A blackbird, says a clear, slightly metallic voice close to my ear. I flinch. I find the voice unpleasant. I want to keep going, but he stops me. City blackbirds have to sing louder to be heard, he says and starts walking. He overtakes me and turns his face toward mine. Unfortunately they've forgotten how to adjust the volume, he continues, they tend to scream. In the late twilight, his eyes look almost brown, but his gaze is just as penetrating as before. He continues up the street, I follow hesitantly. He holds his back unusually straight, almost stiffly, but his arms swing as if they weren't properly attached to his torso. I don't like running after him, so I decide to turn right at the next intersection. We reach the intersection and he turns right. I follow him, as if I'd been found out, along a brick wall, behind which there is a park with tall trees. A light wind sways the branches, which have just sprouted, some have buds, a few are already blooming. He stops at an iron gate. He pushes on the handle. It doesn't give. He takes a running start and leaps onto the wall. When he jumps, he seems to fling his arms out wide and he manages to anchor himself on top of the wall. He stands up straight and in the next moment, he has disappeared on the other side. My heart is hammering in my throat. A few minutes pass and I neither hear nor see a thing: I feel ridiculous, standing there, waiting, for what I don't know, led down the garden path and left behind. I wonder where I could go. With a groan, he throws himself at the wall again, this time from the other side, and grunting, pulls himself up. He stands, looking down at me. I want to show you something, he says and drops to the ground, landing very close to me. He springs back up immediately, leans his back against the wall, clasps his hands and holds them out to me at crotch-height. How are his loose, wobbly arms supposed to lift me? I approach without a word and without looking at him, steady myself on his shoulders, and use his hands as a step to climb effortlessly over the wall.

We're in an old cemetery. The graves and paths are overgrown with grass, only the gravestones assert themselves.

I've already looked for him on this side, he's not there, so let's take a look over there, he says.

I have no idea who he's talking about. Where on earth is my lighter? I must have lost it. Do you have a light? I ask. I don't smoke, he says and kneels down very close to the gravestones. It looks like he's hugging them.

No, not here. Not here either. No. How is this possible? Where can he be?

It doesn't matter to me that I don't know who or what he's talking about. Right now I feel like I'm in such good hands, this could go on forever as far as I'm concerned.

A lovely young woman, he says out of nowhere in a voice suddenly much darker, is being courted by a handsome young knight. A proper love story. Maybe we should give the two of them names, what do you think? Unfortunately, I can't remember. Let's call them Julia and Julius.

He leans against the tombstone. I can feel his piercing gaze on me and bring my hand to my neck, to my collarbone, as if to fend him off.

Before Julia gives Julius an answer, he continues, he must prove himself. She sends him into the sinister forest. This deep, dark forest is infamous. Come, he says and stands up. He walks one step behind me, as if he were driving me forward. We reach the wall and climb over it like an experienced team of thieves.

After several tricky encounters in the forest, he says when we're back on the street, Knight Julius reaches a stretch of land along the river that belongs to a fisherman and his wife. Let's call them Karl and Karla.

We follow the cemetery wall around one street corner and come to a tall entrance gate. I turn away and cross the street, I zig and zag, and decide on a cobbled side street. He follows me.

It's late, he says, and the fisherman and his wife, Karl and Karla, take Julius in for the night. It's raining and the river rises. Finally, the couple's daughter comes home completely drenched. Julius is amazed that Karl doesn't scold his daughter for being out so late and he learns that this young woman—Undine, hers is the only name I can remember—was a foundling and has always been deaf to their advice and commands. She does what she wants, Karl tells him, but we still love her in a strange way. She came to us when our own child was taken by the river. In the morning our daughter fell out of the boat and that evening Undine stood at our door, dripping wet, like she is now. She has lived with us ever since.

Undine? My grandmother had told me many stories about her. You should read that book sometime, she would say, but I never did. Why is this man with husky eyes telling me her story? Am I dreaming? I stop and look at him. He smiles at me. Undine, he says, goes straight to Knight Julius and kisses him on the mouth. I recoil but the stranger continues his story: Julius is breathless for a moment, then seems to have lost his senses. Every thought of Julia is erased. Tell me about the sinister forest, Undine asks and pulls Julius down next to her on the bench, but Karl, who has just fetched a bottle of wine, smacks the table: not in my house! Julius is taken aback. Undine jumps up and runs out the door into the rain.... Should we get a drink? he asks, pausing. We're standing in front of a bar, decorated with strings of colored lights. I could use a glass of wine now, too. I run off.

At the crossroads, I'm out of breath. I brace myself, my hands on my knees, as if breathing were easier that way. *Bakery Pastry Shop* is written in strangely ornate, fecal brown letters on a corner store. Through the plate glass window I see cakes in a display case and then, having raised my eyes only slightly, I see him reflected in the glass, and it looks like he's in the shop, bending over the cakes. Who forgot those there? he asks, that's a proper ghost feast. He begins whistling a jaunty tune that seems familiar, but I can't place it. His gaze meets mine, piercing despite the detour of the display window reflection, keen, stopping at nothing, penetrating every substance. I close my eyes and rest my forehead against the glass.

Look at that, he says when I open my eyes again. It's sprouting again. He rubs his hand over his chin. I shaved only this afternoon. Horrible. I don't want to see you, you hear? Stay out of sight. You upset me. Even if you've grown out of me, I don't know you. I don't want to know you. Go away, get lost, crawl back to where you came from, get it? He turns to face me. It won't answer, just like you, it refuses to speak to me. Before a smile can flit across my face, I turn around and walk away.

Undine, he calls after me, Undine, come back! Why do you want to go out in the storm? He catches up with me. The river has overflowed its banks, he says breathlessly. Knight Julius finds Undine on a patch of land in the middle of the flood. He promises to tell her all his adventures in the sinister forest and brings her home to Karl and Karla. We reach a square with a playground at its center, circle it once and return to the street. It's not clear which of us is leading the other.

Karl shows Julius the way back to the city, he says, but he can't cross the river, which has swollen to a powerful torrent. Julius settles in at Undine's side in Karl and Karla's house. He soon feels at home. They live together peacefully, bound in love, but when the store of wine runs out, they argue. Julius remembers Julia and although he doesn't speak nicely about her—she was domineering and it's her fault he went into the sinister forest in the first place—Undine bites his hand when she hears Julia's name. She later stops the bleeding with repeated kisses, then goes off to get more wine. . . . I'm thirsty, I really am, he says. We pass a large brick building, erected in 1846, a hospital if the sign on the entrance is correct. Built the year he died, he murmurs.

The year he died?

I have such a bad memory, he smacks his forehead. Let's stop in here. He heads toward a bar on the corner. The owner says she's closed. I'm closed, he repeats after her and we smile at each other.

He walks next to me, holding a bottle of wine. The owner was willing to uncork it. Fine, she said, but then disappear, bye, see you.

This is the most expensive wine I've ever drunk, he says, and the most sour. His arm swings, the wine sloshes inside the bottle. The flood, he says, washes an itinerant monk up on Karl's doorstep. After a brief reflection on his resources and the urgency of the situation—as well as a long, silent prayer—the monk decides to marry Julius and Undine. Undine seems very solemn. From a small chest, she takes out magnificent mother of pearl rings that belonged to her parents. I hope it fits, she says and slips the larger one onto Julius' finger. It does indeed, Julius exclaims in amazement. After they're married, Undine is exuberant. The monk advises Julius, despite his love for her, to always treat his wife with caution. He advises Undine to bring her soul into line. I don't have one, she says and bursts into tears.

We cross a dark, nearly empty boulevard on which only the streetcar tracks gleam and walk straight toward an imposing Neo-Baroque building, doubtless once a ministry or government building. Its left wing extends along a smaller road, which we follow until we come to a dead-end sign. We keep going, regardless. (We? Yes, we.) Suddenly we're standing on the bank of the Spree. Before us is the tip of Museum Island with an enormous round building, covered in green, apparently undergoing renovation. A bridge leads to the island. We continue walking until we reach the barrier midway across—*Construction zone. Do not enter. Parents are responsible for their children*—and look down into the dark water. After a short silence he picks up his story: The next morning, the flood has receded. Julius decides to leave for the city with Undine. Julia can hardly believe her luck: he's here, Julius is back! The three of them live together in Julius's castle. Julia believes, like everyone else in the city, that Undine is a freed princess. The two women feel bound to each other, without knowing where the feeling comes from.

We stand next to each other at the railing, leaning over it and looking straight down for a while. Then I return to the riverbank and walk along the water, his steps crunch behind me. I feel weightless. The nightlights on the numberless construction cranes shine, isolated but constant; a train viaduct crosses our path, and I wish in vain that a train would thunder across overhead, and when I reach the next bridge, which is flanked to the left and right by two columns that look like candlesticks, I want to ask for another leg up so I could climb onto one of the columns and talk to him, who would be standing on the other, as loud as necessary and as softly as possible. But I remain silent. Are you coming? he asks and I have to pick up my pace to hear the next part of the story.

One day Undine reveals that Julia is actually Karl and Karla's daughter. Julia doesn't want to hear anything about it. Enraged, she rants that she wants nothing to do with these fishermen. Now listen: as proof, Julia's thick hair is lifted. Her ear, her throat, and her shoulders are covered with little dark spots—just like my stubble and just as dense. He interrupts his story and stops for a moment. I have the impression that he's waiting for my response, which remains secret, hidden. I really need to shave soon, he says. Karla, incidentally, recognizes the spots right away, she recognizes her daughter, but she doesn't want Julia anymore and doesn't let her reaction show. . . . What was that?

I threw my ring in the water.

Did you really just say something to me? Was that you? Did you just say you threw your ring in the water?

I don't say anything.

You have a—your voice is really—yes, it's just . . . beautiful.

I don't say anything.

He starts whistling the song he had whistled a few . . . minutes? hours? ago at the bakery storefront. Again, I think I'm just about to recognize it when he alternates between singing and whistling. I realize that I don't know the song at all. I've never heard these lyrics before. *Let stray dogs howl* . . . he whistles . . . *Love loves to wander* . . . he whistles . . . *from one to another*—he stops. He goes up to the river's edge hesitantly and peers into the water, as if hoping to see my ring and then he says: Julia washes herself every day at the castle well, hoping that the well water would wash the spots away. But when Undine has the well sealed with boulders, Julia feels so thwarted, she runs away. Julius follows her and brings her back. Undine does not miss the fact that Julius takes Julia's side more and more often. We reach the landing pier for sightseeing boats. Behind it, the cathedral looms heavy and dark. Since there are no ships anchored here, I wonder where the fleet is docked at night. He sits on the stone steps next to the ticket kiosk and I stand next to him as little waves lap at the quay wall.

The three of them take a trip down the river, he continues his story, and the current grows stronger by the minute, the water wilder, torrential. The ship lists. Julius orders Undine to do something, but she can't calm the waves. Julius lets slip a curse. With a sob Undine falls overboard and sinks under the waves. He starts whistling again, then singing: *from one to another,* and then *my dearest, good night.* I feel a chill in my heart. A quick, icy blast of wind blows through me. I want to climb the steps back onto the promenade, but he grabs my wrist and puts a finger to his lips. I freeze. A bird whistles a long, extended, wistful melody, faster and faster until the song gets muddled and ends in a kind of sob. I think of the blackbird in the twilight. Oh please, it's a nightingale, he says. He can read minds.

I scale the stairs and keep going. Since I don't hear any footsteps, I turn my head. Nice that you're wondering where I am, he says a few steps behind me and after a short silence, he continues his story: In the beginning Undine would come to the knight in dreams, then less and less often. At first, his dreams are varied and colorful and they leave him filled with longing. With time, there is only the same lackluster dream, which he dreads. Undine appears, throws back her wet hair, gives him a piercing look and says: if you marry again, I will have to kill you. That is exactly what Julius plans to do. He wants to marry Julia once the year of mourning has ended. Karla dies and Karl orders his daughter to come to him. She must live with him by the side of the river. That is his wish. Karl objects to the marriage until Julius offers a sum large enough to break his resistance.

Instead of using the pedestrian underpass, I run across a heavily trafficked bridge and stop on the other side. Still standing where I left him, he waves at me.

It is not a light-hearted wedding, he says once he has crossed the bridge. Julia, the bride, is the most pleased and carefree. She makes herself beautiful for the wedding night. She's unable to cover up the pitch-black spots she dislikes so much. After some hesitation, she has the well uncovered. There's no one left to prevent her. It's surprisingly easy. The stone almost rolls itself to the side, as if it were being pushed from underneath.

He crosses his arms and says: it's downright chilly here on the water. Let's walk faster. Trotting, he barely has enough breath to tell his story. The well is barely opened, he pants, when Undine climbs out, dripping wet and weeping bitterly, her hands shielding her face anxiously. Julia freezes. She sees Undine walk hesitantly, as if compelled, with heavy steps toward Julius's chamber.

He hurries on. I'm at his heels. I'd like to grab him by the shoulder and tell him to go on with his story, but I don't. He picks up his pace and the riverbank promenade, lit with lanterns and lined with weeping willows, seems endless. I pick up a stick from the side of the path and hit it against the hip-high wall with every step. He stops and gasps for breath, then continues his story, stopping regularly to catch his breath: When there's a knock on his door, Julius calls out sorrowfully, I'm coming, dearest. The door opens and there is Undine. Here I am, she says. She is divinely beautiful. Julius leans toward her and they kiss. He takes a deep breath. She won't let him go until the last breath has slipped out of him and he sinks from her lovely arms to the floor. He stretches his hand out to me. I kissed him to death, Undine says when the door opens and Julia appears. I shrink back. I can't any more, I say, I can't go another step.

I sit next to him in a taxi. First he had taken me to a nearby subway station and watched me as I slowly realized that no trains were running. He'd smiled at me and called a taxi on his mobile phone. Back to the beginning? he'd asked. I had nodded and got in one side of the taxi, he got in the other and now we're sitting next to each other. The driver turns the radio off. We don't speak.

Regine is sitting at the bar. I recognize her right away. When I poke her from behind, she turns in the wrong direction and sees him first. Hello, Johannes, she says. Hello Regine, he answers. Regine seems happy, but not at all surprised to see me. To see me at his side. Johannes, I say, so your name is Johannes. His eyes are back. His unbelievably piercing, light blue husky eyes. Look at this, he says, pointing at his stubble without taking his eyes from mine, isn't this crazy? He goes to the men's room. Regine smiles at me. Great to see you.

I smile back.

How long have you been in the city?

Since yesterday.

I've already had a bit to drink, she says. I just finished a play this evening.

Fantastic, congratulations, I say. For which theater?

I can't remember the rest of the conversation, even after thinking hard. I do remember how he came back from the men's room, the one who suddenly has a name. He is freshly shaven. Too little light in this hole, he says and pats his cheeks. Will this do? It's like a foreign occupying power. I don't know what he means. I look at Regine. She's talking to the bartender.

Why did you tell me the story? I ask him, the one now called Johannes.

He looks at me, surprised.

Is Julius buried in the cemetery where we were?

Julius is a fictional character, he answers. Julius doesn't have a grave.

I look at him and wonder how long it would take to count his stubble and if it would even be possible.

Julius' spiritual father is in the cemetery, he says, de la Motte Fouqué. At least, that's what I've been told. Hello. . . ?

Yes, I say.

Should we go?

Yes, I say.

I forget to say goodbye to Regine. As soon as we're outside, our conversation ends. We cross the street, turn onto a rising, sparsely tree-lined avenue with a planted median strip and come upon a small, triangular park, without saying a single word. In one corner of the park stands an art nouveau pavilion, painted green, made of metal and, no, not round, but octagonal as becomes clear when we get closer. We circle it and stand in front of the entrance. He knocks on the partition and slips around it into the pavilion. I follow him. The interior is lit by a dim ceiling fixture and the light of the streetlamps shining through the skylights. It takes my breath away. The smell of urine is no less caustic when I breathe through my mouth. I gasp for air and stumble toward him, the one I've known as Johannes for an hour now, and he moves toward me. We meet in the center, open our mouths, and go at each other.

This urinal has seven walls, a circle of seven men could relieve themselves standing shoulder to shoulder. On each wall there are two sensor-activated nozzles that spray the wall after each use. It becomes clear that they are infrared sensors, set off whenever a body stands before them for a while and then steps away. Because we are moving around a lot, there's always at least one section being sprayed, even when we're leaning against the wall.

I'm pretty sure no one comes into the pavilion while we're there, but if so, they witness a struggle. *Let stray dogs howl.* I don't know if he, the one I've known as Johannes for an hour, is as inexperienced as I am. If he is, he doesn't let it show. His stranger's hands tear at my blouse and shove my skirt up. We push and shove each other from one wall to another as if we were wedged together. *Love loves to wander.* We don't let go of each other, don't let go at all, until we're completely drenched, until the birds start screaming in the breaking dawn, all together, all at once, not pleasantly, violently. Dawn light penetrates the skylights, *My dearest, good night.* And I can't get this melody, this song out of my head.

The melody has chased away the knocking. My headache is finally gone. My husband stands in the doorway with a cup of tea. I fall asleep.

5

What he sees

This was not the plan. The sentence I'd wanted to write here, to write down now, was: And then there was Philipp. Actually, my husband should be next—the name Philipp, by the way, suits him very well. After Johannes comes Philipp. But this fine series of emissaries, my entire chronology of men, is muddled. There's a problem.

Life is not cooperating. It intrudes into my book and grabs at the plot. It's your own fault if you think you can tame, order, channel life by writing, your own fault if you think you can take hold of love, examine, and—above all—understand it!

Oh, Petrus. Now that you're on my mind again, everything is getting out of hand. Philipp, in fact, should come next. And now it's a fruit salad.

Salad? Petrus is still repeating every question.

Let's just say it's a mess.

A mess? It's been one for a long time.

For me, it came out of nowhere!

Just be glad you've noticed, now you can start fighting it.

Shadowboxing at best! It's almost time to pick up the kids. Leave me in peace, Petrus, I have to get ready for this evening.

And he's gone.

Anyone who finds herself, like me, in the unusual position of learning, just moments before giving a reading, that her own husband has gambled away a sum of other people's money equal to an entire year's salary, may very well choose the wrong passage to read.

And so I read the first chapter, called "As fast as a person walks," shortened naturally, because these days you can't expect book lovers to listen to anything for longer than seventeen minutes, even if the one reading is me, that is, someone who has been trained in reading out loud. It's a horrible process, mutilating your own work. First you feed your book until it has a well-proportioned body and legs it can stand on, then you trim off the extremities with a flimsy pen, as if you were wielding a butcher's knife. And if that doesn't do it, you lop off the nose and ears until you're down to seventeen minutes. There are a few rules for a successful reading. The first is "read what is on the page." If you follow this rule, there will be almost no opportunity for your thoughts to wander. This also applies to texts you know well: your own or those you've rehearsed or already delivered more than once. The rule does not say "read what you think is written," but "read what is on the page." And this kind of reading—remember those happy moments in the first years of school when reading still meant deciphering one word at a time—blocks out everything else.

But on this evening, I manage while reading, I don't quite know how, to let certain thoughts that are not on the page float into my mind. Not only that, I'm watching television, that is, I see a kind of test image that wobbles slightly but otherwise doesn't move: a host of creditors, crowded together, standing tall and badly lit. The picture persists, stubborn and static, but all my attempts to zoom in on and identify faces I presume are familiar fail. Whoever believes it's impossible to read and watch television at the same time is wrong. The test image flickers over my text—even when I turn the page. I don't even need to raise my head to stare at it. And I don't, which leads me to break the second rule: "Every few sentences give the audience an attentive glance and count how many are sleeping." Why? you ask. Anyone who has done it knows this simple procedure creates a silent but intensive dialogue with your listeners, a dialogue that draws in every last one. Even the most talented sleepers personally thank you afterward for the wonderful reading and buy a copy of your book. Amazing, yet true.

But I don't dare look up, afraid that the host of creditors has spread out, not only over my text but also throughout the room, and are looking at me reproachfully, calling out: Where's our money?

I don't know.

She doesn't know! the creditors jeer.

He gambled it away, I say or rather my inner voice says, or maybe even someone else. In any case, I hear it loud and clear.

Gambled away! While she watched, cool as you please.

No, I didn't know anything about it.

Give our best to your husband. You have twelve hours to pay us or . . . The host of creditors falls silent, and the picture of them disappears. An unknown photograph of my two children takes its place. What are they playing at? What are my two little boys doing here? Who took this picture, when, and why? I could easily have lost my place or misspoken or both, almost. Astonished, I realize I've kept reading the entire time, maybe a little too fast, maybe with the wrong emphasis here and there, but without missing a beat or stumbling, that much is certain. Because on top of it all, I've also been listening to myself as I read. Someone laughs once, ha!—a truncated joke but still, it seems to work. Isolated, on its own.

But why is "As fast as a person walks" the wrong passage?

Because this is a love story. Because it's about a *first* love, which even those who don't spend much time thinking about matters of the heart recall with glowing eyes and a brimming heart. Because it's clear from this section, even in its mangled, seventeen-minute version, that this love doesn't end happily. Because the public tends to take a first-person narrator for the author and that tendency is even stronger when the author reads her own first-person narrative. Because this winter's tale, in which four people go for a walk in the snow fits the present season so well. It's a cold March night. Winter is taking one last frigid and pitiless stand. The fields are covered with snow, the sidewalks and side streets are icy, the heavily trafficked roads are full of slush, and the Alster River has been frozen over for a few days. My introverted, unhappy delivery may be hardening the audience's inclination to believe the narrator is me into the certainty that here and now, one and only one person is standing before them: the narrator, unhappy in love. And that the entire event is one drawn out wail for love, a cry for help to the men in the room. Where do I get this idea? Just a moment.

Even after I've finished reading, I don't look up. I nod curtly, staring at my feet, then step off the podium and head straight for the bar. I drink red wine, it's free and I'm thirsty. I don't speak with anyone, I drink. When the place closes, I'm driven home and helped up the stairs to my apartment by a gentlemanly acquaintance who takes pity on me. I can't open the front door because the damn key no longer fits. Uncle Günter opens the door and looks at me, astonished. Uncle Günter was watching the boys. You don't look good, he says, you're pale. Lie down, if you can. Or go to the bathroom. Uncle Günter sends my acquaintance away, asks me if it's all right to leave me alone, and drives away, home to Aunt Sigrid.

The next day, there's an email in my inbox. Forwarded from my author's page. A stupid address: yourlook@freenet.de. Remarkably, I open the email. I, who am more afraid of Trojan viruses than a terror attack. With good reason: I back up my work only every few years onto an external hard drive Philipp gave me for Christmas a few months after our wedding. A virus had made my computer self-destruct, taking all my unpublished writing down with it. Philipp doesn't understand why, after that experience, I don't back up my data at least once a week, and I can't explain this either. I forget, there's no time, it makes me nervous, distracts me from what's essential: I have no idea. I reassure Philipp by reminding him how careful I am with outside data, files, and emails. You know I'd rather miss out on something than end up with a problem. And yet, I open the email from yourlook@freenet.de:

It's me. You know who. I think your story is very good. Unfortunately we didn't speak, but our eyes kept meeting. Intense looks. Write me if you want. I'd like that.

He signed a common German name, which I fittingly change to Thomas. I read his email several times and have to laugh. I have a splitting headache from the wine. My eyes. Intense looks. Really? When? Nut-job. I click reply and write: You must be confusing me with someone else.

The phone rings. Uncle Günter. He wants to know how I'm doing, if I've heard any news from Philipp. I don't know if it's because of my hangover, but I get pedantic. What do you mean by *any news*? Are you asking if any creditors have called yet this morning? Are you asking if the mountain of debt has gotten even higher? If something else has come out that Philipp was keeping from me?

Günter stays calm. He just wants to know if Philipp called.

Why?

I'm worried about him.

Don't be.

He's not answering his phone.

Maybe he's in treatment, at a medical appointment, in a meeting, in therapy, what do I know. You should be worried about me.

I am.

Günter, that was a joke! I'm doing fine!

Are the boys at nursery school?

Yes. Of course. I'm sorry, I'm having a bad day. I'll call you later. I hang up and delete *You must be confusing me with someone else* and then type it out again and click *send*. I go shopping. I'm amazed at the prices. Potatoes, which I always buy, cost 2.99 euros. How is it that I never noticed before? Aren't potatoes supposed to be cheap? Poor man's food? Oatmeal, on the other hand, 39 cents! It's a good thing the boys love breakfast porridge, that's what they'll be getting for the next ten to twenty years. I open the mailbox. Five envelopes. They're all addressed to Philipp. I open the first one halfway, then put them all unread into my bag. I don't even want to know. I climb the stairs. The key to the front door fits again. Lucky thing.

yourlook@freenet.de has written. Confused you with someone else? Not a chance! You know which one I am: blond with glasses. Would you like to meet for a cup of coffee?

Reply: I have no idea who you are, dear blond-with-glasses. *Send.*

yourlook@freenet.de: coffee?

Reply: I've got the kids, sorry. *Send.*

I try to work, but the book I'm writing, this book right here, is in a crisis, outcome uncertain. I'm afraid to touch it. So I decide to start something new.

Beginning. Beginning again with you. Every book with you. In the beginning was the word. At my beginning, there's you.

I save the twenty words and close the file.

I open it again and read it one more time. Beginning. Beginning again with you. Every book with you. In the beginning was the word. At my beginning, there's you.

I delete the five sentences, go to the kitchen, make a cup of coffee, and regret pushing *delete.* I try to reconstruct the sentences. I looked at him—where did he get that idea? No idea what he saw. Blond with glasses. Who could that be? I take the mail out of the shopping bag and toss it onto the pile in Philipp's room.

Wait until it's clear! I say to my older son. I pull the younger one out of the way. He starts to cry. I pick him up. The older one comes speeding down the slide on his stomach and lands face-first in the frozen sand. He screams and starts to cry. I put the younger one down and pick up the older one, who is still little. The little little one doesn't want to sit in the sand. He starts to bawl. The big little one has scraped his chin. He's almost inconsolable. A bicyclist rides up to the playground. I recognize him right away. Strange. I really have seen this tall, thin, blond man with large amber-colored, horn-rimmed glasses before. But it could have been anywhere. I have no recollection of the circumstances, the place, time, or occasion. The children are crying. Blondwithglasses gets off his bike and tries to open the gate. Child safety lock, I call, turn and pull at the same time, but he can't figure it out. Calm down now, I say, and the children just scream louder. Somehow he manages to open the gate and pushes his bike through it toward us. The children fall silent. They look at him. They look at me. Do you know him, Mama? the older one asks.

Yes, I answer because I can't really say no, I don't know him even though I arranged to meet him here.

Blondwithglasses looks at me. Yes, we know each other, he says. His voice is husky. He clears his throat. I have a band-aid. He pulls his wallet from his bag and finds the band-aid after a lot of rustling. Do you have a children's band-aid? the big little one asks.

What's that?

For children, a children's band-aid. My son looks at me as if I were forcing him to speak to an idiot. I take the band-aid. Thanks so much, I say and stick it on the big little one's chin. At home I'll draw some dots on it, ok?

No! Flowers!

OK, fine, flowers.

And little stars.

It's a deal.

And Gummi Bears.

I sigh.

I'm Thomas, he barges in and offers his hand to the big little one.

What do you have in your hand? my son asks.

Thomas looks at me helplessly.

Do you have any Gummi Bears?

No, I'm afraid not, Thomas says.

But I saw some, my son contradicts him.

Thomas looks at me. What do I do now? he asks.

Thomas went shopping for me. He carried a case of bottled water up to the third floor. He took out the garbage and put the newspapers in the recycling bin. Swept the gravel from the stairs. Brought up the mail. Patched the bicycle tires. Walked the dog. Mailed letters. Returned books. And all this after only one meeting, during which he asked several times if I weren't too nice to my children. It was obvious that he wished they weren't there. That they weren't constantly interrupting, constantly wanting to be picked up or to get my attention. When they're finally asleep, he pokes me with his finger. I raise my head and smile. He takes off his glasses. Now I can't see you anymore, he says. Then I don't need to smile at you anymore, I answer. He puts his glasses back on, looks at me, and says: Now that, I don't get.

The next morning he's at the door with fresh rolls and the newspaper. He takes care of everything that needs taking care of while I close my office door and unplug the telephone and start work on the *Beginning* text. After Thomas has said goodbye, I take a break. I drink an entire bottle of water. I look through the mail. I put the letters to Philipp on the pile in his room. One is addressed to the big little one, that one I can open, how could it be bad news? An account withdrawal. There are only 1.70 euros left in his savings account. I yell. I dial the number. I scream at Philipp over the phone. I scream when I tell Günter about it. I call my friend Nathanael and scream until I weep. I lie down next to the dog on the floor and press my face into her fur. The telephone rings. It's Thomas. I can't speak I'm so angry.

He comes over when the children are asleep. He hugs me without a word and I bite his thin upper arm until I have no strength left in my jaws. He nods. Let it all out, he says and groans with pain.

That was good, he says later, I thought it was good. I'm not sure what he means: that I bit him? Good from the point of view of psychological hygiene? Or because he thinks I've gotten over my rage that way? I haven't. But I have to admit, I also found it good, although I can't explain why I did it. I never bite, otherwise.

I'd like to see you naked, he says.

Why? I ask and, as I'm saying it, think: stupid question.

Because I think you're beautiful, but I only believe what I see.

I shake my head.

Good, he says and starts in. He takes off his clothes in my kitchen. He does it very quickly. His clothes lie behind him like a blurry shadow on the laminated kitchen floor. All Thomas has on are his horn-rimmed glasses. He is standing up straight. He's thin, very pale-skinned, completely hairless, and covered with blue, purple, green, and yellow spots. My teeth marks on his upper arm are dark red.

Where did you get all those bruises?

I'll tell you later. Are you going to take off your clothes?

No. I stay seated. I look at him. Because of their different colors, it's not possible that the bruises all came from one incident or accident or assault. It looks bad, I say. My dog trots into the kitchen, stops behind Thomas, stretches her neck, and sniffs at him. Thomas leaps around, startled. Stop it, you repulsive creature! I have to laugh and pull the dog away. What did she do?

Sniffed. Why "she"?

She's female.

He sits down quickly and crosses his legs. I find his smooth, white legs, his child's chest, his bare groin, unpleasant. His grayish member is tucked between his legs. It almost hurts to think about it.

I'd rather get dressed again, he says, the dog scares me.

He leaves a few minutes later. He says he can't come help tomorrow, he has an important appointment. When I tell him I don't need any help, he strokes my hair and smiles.

On the way to the nursery school, the big little one wants to hold the dog's leash. Nice and slow and watch out for the ice, I say. And wait at the intersection, right? The dog lunges forward. The boy lets himself be pulled along, and I run behind with the little little one in the stroller, which makes the dog run faster and, dragging behind her, the child. Stop! I yell, but they're still running, running across the street, faster and faster. The child is laughing, the child slips and falls flat. I sit on the cold asphalt, scold the dog, and comfort the child. Tears stream down my face. They're strangely warm.

Philipp calls. The answering machine picks up after four rings. I push the speaker button. I'm afraid I'm going to lose you, I hear Philipp say. Please call me when you get home.

I erase the message.

I can't think straight. I'm sitting at my desk, working on the *Beginning* text, again. I'm hardly making any progress. *I, You, Dialogue,* it says.

I: I don't believe it.

You: I believe you do.

I: Do you?

You: I do.

Period, I write. End of dialogue. *I only believe what I see.* I think of Thomas.

Why are we here? the big little one asks. We're going ice-skating, I tell him.

For ice cream? He looks at me incredulously.

Ice-skating.

Where's the ice? he asks. Right here! We're standing on it. I stamp my foot.

I'm cold.

I'm cold, too. It's a greedy cold that spreads within minutes up from the ground and numbs the feet, calves and legs up to the knees, then creeps relentlessly and purposefully up the thighs to the rear end and insides.

I want to go home, Mama.

So do I, sweetheart. My phone rings. Thomas wants to cook us dinner. He already went shopping and is on his way to our house. Actually, he's already on the doorstep. It's downright chilly, he says. We'll hurry, I say and hang up.

Are they asleep?

I nod.

Today it's your turn, he says when he has finished washing up and sat down next to me.

No, you were going to give me some answers first.

Like what?

Like how you were abused.

Abused?

Got those bruises.

Other questions?

I think it over.

Do you not have any hair on your body or did you shave it off? I ask.

Shaved it.

Everywhere?

He nods.

What for?

He smiles and suggests we play a game: I ask questions and he'll give answers. After each question, I have to take off a piece of clothing.

But I can ask whatever I want, I demand, and you have to answer.

It's a deal, he says. And so I end up doing the first striptease of my life. I stand in front of him.

Thomas, how old are you?

Almost thirty.

(I take off a sock.)

Marital status?

Single.

(Second sock.)

Children?

None.

(Cardigan.)

Why not?

Because I've never slept with a woman without using a condom.

You've never—?

Never. That was two answers.

(Protesting, I take off my scarf and my pants. I count how many pieces of clothing I still have on. I have to get to the essential questions.)

No beating around the bush: Who do you have sex with?

He gives a laugh. All right then, fine, why not get straight to the point. I have profiles on two dating sites. I request meetings with women. But that rarely works, it's not—he smiles—reliable. And so, when I'm in the mood, I go to a hookup bar, you know what that is?

Now you've asked me a question. No, I don't.

All sorts of people go, couples, men, women, to live it up sexually. Unfortunately, women are usually in the minority, so for men, there's no guarantee we'll be admitted.

I'm beginning to like this game. When have I ever gotten such candid answers, especially from a man? He's telling me how he goes to some places where he gets as close, physically, to complete strangers as two people possibly can. Wow! I pull my T-shirt off over my head.

Do your bruises have something to do with your visits to these bars?

More with meetings through the dating sites.

I try to hide my astonishment. I unhook my bra quickly and without fuss.

It doesn't seem all that *unreliable*. Judging by the number of bruises, you can't be doing all that badly on the dating sites. That wasn't a question!

I only have my panties on. I don't have any more questions, I say.

Don't you want to know how I got the bruises?

Yes. No. That is, yes, but I'm not going to ask, I say.

After a short pause he asks, Do you not like taking your panties off?

No.

He comes up to me and puts his arms around me.

Go ahead and bite if you want, he says.

No, I answer and pick my clothes up off the floor.

But I really like what I see, he says.

I have no idea what you see with your funny-looking glasses, I say and pull my T-shirt on, over my head. Can I look through them?

He takes off his glasses, wipes the lenses with his sleeve, and hands them to me.

They hurt my eyes. Everything is distorted. I take them off.

Thomas, at the reading . . .

Yes?

I didn't look at you once the entire evening.

I thought you did.

No.

That's what it felt like to me.

I didn't. Do you set up a new email address to fit every woman you meet? Like yourlook@freenet.de?

No, I've had that one for a while, at least a few years.

So that means you write other women using that address?

Not at the moment.

He had planned a dessert that still needed some preparation: pears poached in red wine. I brew some coffee. He tells me he's brought his portfolio, he has been wanting to show me some of his work for a while, so that I can get some idea of what he's *up to* all day.

I leaf through his file of information graphics while he constantly stirs the red wine to dissolve the sugar. The public busing network in Schleswig Holstein. The structure and paths of swine flu contagion. A diagram of all the forces that set off the global bank crisis. Visual perception is the primary means of information intake in humans. That's the source of infographics' power and their advantage over other forms of journalism. He sums it up with the catchy saying: A picture says more than a thousand words. He turns down the flame, leaves the pot to simmer, and looks over my shoulder. To put it simply: his job is to make complicated connections visible in such a way that they can be grasped in a single glance.

He takes the pot off the burner. The pears are delicious.

Before leaving, he asks: Should I come back tomorrow to help?

Better not tomorrow, I answer.

He goes out the door without saying goodbye.

I get undressed, climb into bed, and think of Philipp, that is, I try to think of Philipp, but can picture only a pair of large, amber-colored, horn-rimmed glasses and when I take them off, Petrus's face appears. He looks at the space between my eyebrows and asks the question I'd asked only in my thoughts. Glasses? No, I don't wear glasses. Especially not to bed. I turn onto my stomach, close my eyes, and hold my breath.

6

Sham couple

Love, Nathanael says and then, after a long pause during which he doesn't take a breath, enough already! We trudge through the sparse Buxtehude Forest in the rain, looking for his mother's grave. Nathanael's mother isn't dead, she's just suffering from dementia, but her husband, Achim, is already planning her burial. To be fair, he's planning his own, too, and even his girlfriend Julika's, because according to his plan, they will all be buried at the foot of the same tree in the Buxtehude Forest, where Julika's husband, Fredi, already lies.

Fredi died suddenly five years ago at the age of seventy-five without any sign of illness, and for several thousand euros, Julika had rented space under the tree for thirty years as a companion grave, expandable for up to eight people. The corresponding contract with the firm that offers such forest interment is kept in Julika's safe, the breadbox in the kitchen where she had stored documents and cash for years, instead of the crusty rolls Fredi so loved. "Expandable up to eight people." Julika, and only Julika, will decide who can lie with Fredi. She, herself, of course. That leaves six more places. Since she and Achim became a *loving couple*—their relationship progressed in parallel with his wife's dementia—Julika has decided that, as things stand, Achim should have one of the places, namely, the one right next to her. Achim thinks the idea is essentially a good one, though he doesn't plan on dying any time soon. Furthermore, he thinks Julika should concentrate on earthly pleasures instead of eternity. However, because he is also keen on having all these unhappy final matters decided once and for all, he listened to her plan attentively. But, my dear Julika, he said after a moment's thought, I can't possibly plant poor Gisela somewhere all by herself. What do you think, could she be buried there, too? Then Fredi wouldn't be so alone either. And then later, when we join them, the two of them wouldn't need to feel so jealous. Seems to me like a good solution for everybody. Achim didn't have the slightest doubt that his wife, Gisela, would die soon, and obviously long before him and Julika. In the end, Julika agreed. Nothing was said to Gisela. Why bother her with a decision like that, Achim said, since she doesn't understand anything anymore?

Still, before Gisela's name is given to the forest internment company, Achim wants to obtain his son's consent. And so Nathanael and I are walking through the forest on this rainy April morning, the wet ground sagging beneath our feet, looking for an ash tree marked with a small cross on a map that Nathanael is constantly folding and unfolding. All the while, he explains the intricate relationships in his family's older generation until my head starts to spin. There is a counter-couple to Achim and Julika, namely Wolf and Bärbel, Nathanael's uncle and his girlfriend. But you don't really want to know about them, he says after he'd explained everything in great detail, infatuated seniors, horrifying! But, anyway, love . . . (long pause, no breath) enough already. I'm glad I'm done with it.

Nathanael is my closest friend. Originally he was Philipp's closest friend. They'd met ten years ago on a train. Nathanael liked Philipp so much that he wanted to spend time with him, even though it was immediately clear that any erotic advances would be futile. They became friends, even though they had no interests in common, other than cooking. They gave each other books and music, even though their tastes were incompatible. For the most part, they disliked each other's gifts and discussed their dislike openly, but did not get discouraged and kept offering gifts in the hope of finding at least one book or one song they agreed on.

I met Nathanael soon after Philipp and I married, after he had returned from an extended stay in Africa. Had he been around, Philipp would certainly have asked Nathanael to be his best man. Nathanael was in a bad state and Africa couldn't have helped him with that. Still, he beamed when he saw us and greeted us with the words: Verily, verily, I say unto you, you are a beautiful couple! His longtime lover, Angelo, had left him earlier. Angelo had forged Nathanael's signature on some bungled financial transactions and caused enormous losses. He had still found time on the run to pack up all of Nathanael's bank and credit cards, traveler's checks, cash, and watch before he disappeared. Nathanael thought he was going to lose his mind. At least the well-digging project in Namibia spared him that. Nonetheless, when he returned six months later, his misery had not diminished.

What does an ash tree look like, actually? Nathanael asks after we'd walked in circles and crisscrossed the forest for an hour. The canopy isn't very thick. He shakes his wet head and I jump away to avoid the fine spray. I'm sorry, he says, I can't read this map. I don't understand it.

Aren't ash trees particularly tall? I ask.

Look up, Nathanael says, they're all tall.

They have ridged bark, I think.

You think? Nathanael echoes. And probably green leaves as well, right? We look at each other. Imagine, if I let them bury my poor, old mother here, I'll never find her again! He looks around. Ash tree, he hisses. Ash-sh-sh. He bares his teeth.

Nathanael and I liked each other at first sight. I liked the music he listened to, he liked the books I read. Cooking was the only thing we couldn't do together. He refused to eat the foods I liked and vice versa. Philipp would leave us—his best friend and his wife—alone anywhere but in the kitchen. Let me man the stove, otherwise there won't be anything to eat or one of you will get hurt, maybe even both of you.

When Nathanael heard that Philipp had gambled away all our money, even the children's savings, he cried. And what do we do now? He blew his nose. Where is Philipp?

In the rehab clinic.

Good Lord! Why there?

Because he has a gambling addiction, Nathanael.

Oh good Lord! And I can't leave here right now.

Fortunately, he had put in for a vacation in two weeks when his father would take Julika to the Black Forest. During the day, he would take care of his mother, who had been hospitalized after a fall down the stairs. The evenings he would spend with us, playing with the children, putting them to bed, cooking with me.

You really want to cook with me?

Absolutely.

A strong wind picks up. We didn't bring any jackets and are freezing in our rain-drenched sweaters. Nathanael looks at me apologetically. He's sorry to have dragged me along on this horrible excursion, through this pathetic forest, in completely unsuitable weather, he tells me. Where is spring anyway? He collapses against a tree trunk. How I loathe this forest! Just like I despise all forests. Every goddamn crap forest in the whole area. The trees aren't the worst of it. There are all the damn animals. I hate them all, the bunnies and wild boar and deer and martens and raccoons and dormice, everything you can shoot at, what you can bag and gut and skin and butcher and roast and eat—by the way, where's your dog?

Here.

Put her on the leash.

Why?

If you don't, they'll shoot her and then claim they took her for a fox.

Nonsense, I say.

They're all in, Nathanael replies. My father is a hunter, his father was a hunter, and his brother Wolf was the best hunter of them all. It runs in our family. Though I don't know what went wrong in my case.

But hunting season's closed.

My ass. There's no closed season for hares and foxes. And raccoons and raccoon dogs are exempted in April.

He turns away. I walk up close behind him. He's gasping for breath. I open my arms wrap them around his chest. His heart is racing, his breathing is uneven.

Once I watched my father skin a raccoon dog. It whimpered with its last strength. My father skinned it alive. It's easier that way, he said. The raccoon dog was still warm. Back when Angelo left, I'd wake in a panic in the middle of the night. I saw my skin hanging off me in shreds and all I could do was whimper like the raccoon dog. Nathanael took a deep breath. Have you ever heard a raccoon dog?

No. I didn't even know there was such a thing.

They look a little like raccoons. As pups, they make these barely audible whimpers, but the young males give these long, drawn-out howls at night when looking for their lifemates. Nathanael howls, frees himself from my hug, turns to face me, and gives a sharp laugh. I'll never be able to love anyone again, he says. Give me a robot, for all I care, it wouldn't bother me at all that it's a machine, just the opposite, I would like that. Nothing from any orifice, no glands, no secretions, no odors, wonderful. No bodily imperfections, no deterioration. There. And now let's find that damn grave.

There are no indications whether a tree is a grave marker or not. There are no commemorative stones, no inscriptions, no names. A few scattered trees have blue or yellow bands around their trunks. Nathanael supposes they're ones that haven't been sold yet. This would mean, on the other hand, that most trees are already taken.

So many corpses here, I say, but Nathanael explains that the dead are cremated before being buried at the foot of their tree-graves.

Too bad. I was picturing the foxes and martens at their nightly feasts.

Nathanael gives me a disapproving look. You mean they'd dig up the bodies and eat them?

Of course. My dog goes straight for any carrion, why shouldn't the forest animals?

Nathanael sighs.

Why do things always have to become unappetizing so quickly? Since we're on the topic, there's something else I wanted to tell you about Wolf and Bärbel. I forgot the most important part! He stops and slips the map into his pocket. I've had it, he says. OK with you if we give up?

On the way back I ask Nathanael what he'll decide. He looks out the window and thinks it over. What would I do if I were he? He lives in Berlin. If he wants to visit his mother's grave, he'll have to go another hour by train from the Hamburg station to Buxtehude and then run through the forest, assuming, of course, that the ash tree really does exist and that he can remember its location. But how often does anyone visit his dead mother anyway? I try to picture his father in the Black Forest with his girlfriend. I wonder what kind of canoodling they get up to. Nathanael smiles at me. Hey, where are you? he asks.

How did your father meet Julika?

They've lived next-door to each other for forty years.

And they've been together that long?

No, of course not. Only since my mother didn't understand anything anymore.

Was your mother friends with her before? Or with Julika's husband?

Not at all. They couldn't stand each other.

And now they're supposed to lie in the same grave?

Exactly.

You can't do that to your mother.

No, I can't, can I?

Nathanael drives straight from the forest to the hospital to see his mother. I go home. Philipp left me a message. He misses the children. And me. Even if I don't want to hear it. And he has news: he will likely get out in ten days. And then? How does he think it will go? I need some distance, I write him. I've barely sent the message when the phone rings. Philipp sobs into my ear. I tell him I'm sorry, but I can't talk right now. I hang up.

Nathanael puts the boys to bed. I hear him whistling the sandman song, then he says in a deep voice: Children dear, pay close attention, I've got something worth the mention. He starts telling them a story, but is interrupted every few seconds. He lowers his voice, he raises it, but no matter what he does, the children are all worked up. Stop! he shouts, or I'll throw sand at you. Silence. Nathanael continues his story. I think the boys are asleep but then the older one comes into the kitchen, crying.

Thanatal threw sand in my eyes! Now they're broken. I can't see anything.

Then we'll have to wash them out.

No! It hurts!

Nathanael appears in the kitchen door.

Nathanael, did you throw sand? I ask severely.

No, he answered, I only sprinkle sand when you're already asleep, so you can see your dreams better. Or would you rather not see them at all?

I do want to! the big little one shouts. He takes Nathanael's hand and pulls him back to the bedroom.

We don't cook, of course we don't, since Philipp isn't here to intervene should peace be jeopardized. We agree that we're not at all hungry, drink sweet tea, and nibble on crisp bread. Nathanael is very quiet. My mother's arm has been sewn up like a cabbage roll, he finally says, sweeping the crumbs from the table with the flat of his hand. The color fits, too, her arm is all yellow-violet. The physical therapist gave her a compliment, said how well-coordinated she is for someone her age. And she answered proudly that after thirty years of yoga, it's hardly surprising. Nathanael stands up and drops the crumbs into the garbage can, then washes his hands and sits back down. He reaches for another slice of crisp bread. Then, when I was alone with her, my mother didn't know what to say for a long time. I think it made her uncomfortable. Finally she said: I could get you some chocolate from the cellar. Next time, please call before you visit, I want to be sure I'm here. That I'm not at work. Some crumbs fall from his mouth. He apologizes, sweeps them with the flat of his hand into his other hand as he had earlier, stands up, and shakes his hands over the garbage can, looks at his palms, goes over to the sink, and washes them. He steps up to the window. Outside it's already dark. I think it's raining again. After that endless winter, constant rain. Oh well, he sighs. My father can't manage. He designed and built the house himself decades ago and now he lives there all alone and refuses to move. Living next door to Julika is convenient, but the yard work, the housekeeping, the laundry. Buying groceries, cooking, cleaning, he didn't do any of it his entire life. At the most, he grilled a steak now and then, hunter that he was. Now he cooks potatoes and puts in way too much salt. He was slicing turnips and had an attack of gout. What are you doing, fixing yourself rabbit food? I asked. He laughed and was proud of himself and of me. But in the middle of the flare up, when I asked how he was doing, he shouted at me: I'm doing fine! He fought against the pain. But Irm is dead, he said to me. What do you mean, dead? I asked. She's dead, she just dropped dead. Irm is, or was, his brother's wife. My father's pain gradually eased. She wasn't even old, what do I know, heart attack. All she ever ate were those biscuits.

She just wore herself out. And Wolf? My father laughed contemptuously, Wolf! He's letting loose. He was taking a cure with Bärbel at the time. He had taken up with his old girlfriend again, from back when he was younger, this Bärbel. I know her from way back, very sensuous, always liked to eat. Not like Irm with her biscuits. And my dear brother didn't even interrupt his cure. Cremated and into an unmarked grave went poor Irm. Horrible. Lying out there somewhere. And that is not going to happen to Mother, you understand, my boy. She should be laid to rest properly. What's nicer than a forest? What is more peaceful? She should lie there next to Fredi.

My little son is standing there, the big little one. Which Fredi? he asks. He had a dream. I saw something! It's not easy to understand what exactly. A huge backhoe with wings? And you were the backhoe driver? No, the pilot. I see. And flew way up in the sky, then fell back down. And then? The end, my son says. I want to again. Thanatal, can you throw sand in my eyes again?

When Nathanael comes back into the kitchen, I remind him that he wanted to tell me something else about Wolf and Bärbel. The two of them are an unusual couple, I think it's fair to say, Nathanael says, and asks if there is any more crisp bread. Bärbel was a chubby girl and back then, after the war, that was rare. Because Wolf liked her, he started slipping her food. Usually it was a piece of bread or an apple, whatever he could spare. Over time he started giving her his whole snack, everything his mother gave him, even the extra piece of bread she slathered with schmaltz because he was so thin and was good at wheedling things out of her. Wolf brought more and more, but it was never enough. The crisp bread snaps loudly and Nathanael laughs. Wolf watched Bärbel as she ate, but as soon as she had swallowed the last bite, the hunger pangs started again. Wolf did what he could. Bärbel blossomed and as her waistline grew, so did Wolf's love for her. Bärbel matured early and let Wolf touch her breasts when he gave her something sweet. Later, she let him suck on them, too.

When they were caught, fat Bärbel was standing stark naked on a crate, her legs spread, scarfing down a sausage sandwich while Wolf was sticking one key after another, on a large ring, into her vagina, as deep as it would go. They were twelve. Their parents forbade them all contact. They kept meeting, every year finding increasingly clever hiding places. Bärbel became pregnant when she was seventeen. Wolf was the one who noticed the child's movements. By then Bärbel was already in the sixth month. Her parents stuck her in a home, the child was taken away as soon as it was born. Bärbel didn't even know if it was a boy or a girl. She wrote Wolf several letters but they didn't reach him, so she never got an answer. Nathanael drains his tea in one gulp, reaches for another piece of crisp bread, and says: I just can't stop!

Wolf and Bärbel didn't see each other again for decades. He went to college, got his hunting license, married Irm, had a daughter, and tried without success to *produce* a son. Irm endured it, but didn't enjoy it. She managed to avoid a second pregnancy—how she did remains her secret. Fat Bärbel married twice and, after several miscarriages, had a son. When she went to visit her first grandchild in the hospital—she was retired by then—an agitated Wolf was standing at the reception desk repeating again and again: My name is Wolfgang Fendel and I'd like to know what room my wife, Irmgard Fendel, née Kraushaar, is in; she was admitted today with a case of renal colic. Hello, Wolf, it's me, Bärbel, Bärbel said behind him. You're thin now, Wolf said. Now you're exaggerating, Bärbel said, patting her stomach and hips. It's great to see you. They've been inseparable since. Only Irm stood between them. But they were both experienced in secrecy. Wolf immediately got busy putting meat on her bones. OK, that'll do, Nathanael says and folds up the crisp bread package. Bärbel is now so fat that she can't get off the sofa without help. She just sits all day long and eats whatever Wolf fixes and serves her. As for Wolf, he's as gaunt as ever, a tall, narrow-shouldered man with sparse, silver hair and wireless glasses, who stuffs his love until she bursts or until she suffocates. Or just can't any more. Until she succumbs, is extinguished. Wolf is a hunter, as you know. He has experience in bringing down prey. Nathanael stands up. He nods to himself, looks at the ground, and seems to be thinking something over. Think of all the trouble I'll be spared, now that I've given up on love, he says and pauses indecisively for a moment. I'll check on the kids, he says. Don't forget the sand, I call after him.

The next morning, the big little one is running a fever. I fell down, he whines. It was just a dream, I tell him, but he objects: I fell down, Mama, my head hurts.

Nathanael takes the little little one to nursery school. Sand will give you wild dreams, I say when he returns. The big little one says that he flew very high, to the far end of heaven and fell from way up there. Nathanael doesn't think it was a dream. And what if he fell out of bed last night. We should have a doctor check him.

The pediatrician's waiting room is completely full. My son plays tag with another little patient. If he's not sick now, he'll catch something here, I think. A continuous stream of new mothers and children arrives, an occasional father as well. One mother, still wearing her rain-soaked jacket, sits next to me. Hello, she says. Hello, I answer, wouldn't you rather hang up your coat?

I was worried the seat next to you would be taken right away, she says. She looks at Nathanael. Hello, she says, I'm Silke.

The wife of the witness at our marriage, I whisper when she finally gets up to hang up her coat after I promised her three times I would save her seat.

Do you know each other? Nathanael is clearly irritated.

No, why?

Just asking. He picks up a brochure with the title *Proper dental hygiene from the very beginning* and reads it with absorption.

Silke asks me how I'm doing, I say fine and ask her the same. Silke asks what's wrong with the little one. I explain that we don't know yet and ask her the same. Silke asks no more questions and that's a bad sign. When Nathanael goes outside briefly without saying why, Silke says: Things sure have changed with you two! I'd already heard.

Help me out, Silke, I reply, what has changed with us?

Silke blushes. Eyes wide, she stammers, well . . . and looks at the door, through which Nathanael left.

I'm sorry, Silke, I don't get it, I say, although I do. She thinks Nathanael is my new boyfriend. Silke must have heard that Philipp is in rehab and thought she was putting two and two together. Silke is the stupidest person I have met in the last twenty years. I give her a friendly smile. Please, Silke, help me out, go ahead and say it.

Oh, nothing.

Go ahead, please.

No.

Then I'll tell you, Silke dear, and this will be the last sentence you'll ever hear me say to you, so pay close attention: Philipp and I are married, as you should know since you were presumptuous enough to come to our wedding reception without being invited. We had wanted to celebrate very privately with just our two witnesses and there's probably no point in explaining, but since that day Philipp and I share the same name, the same worries, the same responsibilities—and now, good luck to you.

Nathanael walks back through the door, sits next to me without a word, and picks up the brochure again. I'm here, he says.

We were just taken for a couple, imagine.

How cute, he says, and leafs through the brochure.

On the way home he wants to hear it again and again even though he'd been standing in the waiting room doorway, listening. And you really said, *pay close attention*?

I did, I learned it from the Sandman last night and wanted to use it right away.

We both laugh. Stop, my son says, you're making my head hurt. The pediatrician had looked into his eyes and said that since he couldn't see into his head, he had to ask a few questions.

Where does it hurt?

My head!

And where, show me.

Here, and here, and here, and here, my son said and circled the entire globe on his shoulders with his index finger.

Does it hurt all the time or just sometimes?

It hurts!

That's often how it is, the pediatrician said, the parents need me, not the children. He offered his hand: Goodbye.

But what's wrong with him? I asked.

We'll have to wait. It's definitely not a concussion. Keep an eye on him. If he complains of nausea or becomes apathetic, bring him back to see me.

So we're a sham couple then, Nathanael says softly since we've stopped laughing out of consideration for my son's headache.

We walk along the canal. The rain has stopped. The wind rustles the leaves and drops trickle down.

Looking around, at least we make a pretty good couple, he says.

It's just a shame we can't cook together, I reply.

Nathanael continues determinedly. I don't think so, he says. Look at it this way: Wolf and Bärbel are perfectly in tune culinarily, but you wouldn't necessarily want to trade places with them. Or the cannibal who always serves his lover special dishes, the ones that make flesh especially tender . . .

What's a cannibal? my son asks.

That's enough, I say, could my sham partner please change the subject?

Thanatal, what's a cannibal?

Could my sham partner please make a bit more of an effort? I ask.

My sham partner could help me out a bit, he says.

Mama, what is it? What's a cannibal?

A man-eater, we call out simultaneously, in irritation.

Oh, my son says and falls silent.

We all remain silent for a time. My son falls asleep in the stroller.

Nine more days, I say. Nathanael nods. Philipp is coming home in nine days. Nathanael throws me a sidelong glance and asks, can we take what you said to Silke as a decision?

In my mind, I'm always writing him contradictory messages. Please find somewhere to stay. / I'm looking forward to seeing you. / I'm afraid—well, that much I'd never admit. I haven't sent any of the messages yet. I come to a stop. Oh, look at that. I think that's an ash.

Why do you think that? Nathanael can sound very skeptical.

Because I looked it up in my tree book after our walk yesterday. That's an ash tree.

Nathanael studies it for a long time. He circles it twice. He takes hold of the trunk. He strokes the bark with his hands. He leans against it.

It's lovely, he says. We should take this one. What do you think? He waits until I look at him, and then winks at me.

7

Just poof, *out of nowhere*

They say that once you get over the initial shock, things are fine again. For me, it was the opposite. The real, deep horror set in only after a few weeks, but then with such force that I didn't know what to do other than play dead. I didn't write a thing, not a single sentence. I listened a lot, listened inside myself, listened to the world outside, but heard nothing, not even Petrus's voice although I thought of him often. No *Come on, keep going!* Nothing, not even the annoying knocking. For three whole months.

In the meantime, summer had come. I was completely unprepared for the heat. In the constant April showers, I'd gotten used to putting on a trench coat before leaving the house. A week ago, or was it two, the heat hit me one morning, and a woman looked at me, shaking her head.

And otherwise? Philipp came home, he swore, he begged, he was combative and hopeful. I said nothing because I didn't know what to say.

Love is not something you choose, dear heart, is the sentence I thought of most frequently during those three months. And the gesture I made most often was to touch my left cheek. Grandmother, heart, Philipp. Suddenly he was there.

The way I picture it, the director had said, is that you appear back there, just *poof,* out of nowhere. The forestage inclined sharply downward. In the back, the stage was about two meters high. I can climb up there, I replied, but I'm sorry to say I can't fly.

It was our first stage rehearsal. I was part of the team working on the first production under the new management. We'd rehearsed for weeks with a mock-up of the stage set and had had to imagine the ramp. That afternoon we were breaking new ground on two fronts. The opening stage set felt foreign. The theater was completely so. Its history was as celebrated as it was uneven. The best had succeeded, all the others had failed. The theater was renowned for its terrible acoustics and an enormous seating area, the full depths of which you couldn't sense from the stage. At that moment it was completely empty except for a few seats in the parterre occupied by the directing team. Still, stagehands, prop men, lighting technicians, and make-up artists, even a few ladies and gentlemen from the administration, the management, and the marketing department had crowded into the wings to see what the new team was up to.

The director cut the next attempt short without giving me a glance by calling out to the stage manager: Could you send someone over here? And a stagehand hurried over in a crouch, even though the ramp was so high, he wouldn't have been visible to the audience standing up straight. Head ducked, knees deeply bent, he headed toward me swiftly and silently. He reminded me of a cat, so that even today, I still picture a black cat creeping up to me. He knelt on one knee and gestured at me to stand on the other. He put both hands on my hips and stood up, so that I, with arms outspread, ready to embrace the world, appeared to rise weightlessly at the edge of the ramp: I floated. Fantastic, the director shouted, and there was applause from backstage and the wings, yes, even from the fly loft. Quiet please, called the director, unsettled by signs of life from a source she couldn't see or control, and back to the script! I played the next scene hovering along the edge of the ramp to see what the stagehand was doing. He left as he had come: creeping silently in a crouch.

While changing clothes after the rehearsal, I looked at myself in my underwear in the mirror, as if I were searching for traces of his hands on my hips. He'd grabbed me forcefully without any shyness. It was both pleasant and embarrassing, especially at the moment when he stood up and my rear end passed in front of his face and hovered above him and I had the feeling he could see right through me from below all the way up to my skull.

Unfortunately, my levitating entrance was cut as I learned the next day at the beginning of the rehearsal. It doesn't fit the play, the director said. What would the message be? That your character brings more than what is earthly and tangible? It's precisely her palpability and earthiness that make her powerful and erotic. Let's give up this hint of the supernatural and concentrate on the sensuous, right?

I didn't see him for days. After one rehearsal I heard the announcement: *Tech please come to the stage for alterations. Alterations, please.*

The seats were dark. I slipped into a loge in the second tier and watched. He worked quickly and with great concentration; now and then he paused and made jokes I couldn't catch. I heard him laugh with his colleagues.

A few days later, he came up to me in the cafeteria.

Excuse me, would you happen to have a cigarette?

No, sorry.

Then it's all good.

Good?

I only smoke when I'm embarrassed.

I had to laugh.

Can I introduce myself: Philipp. My friends call me Philipp.

Hello, Philipp.

My enemies, too, by the way.

Ah, yes.

At home, they also said Philipp, earlier.

How about that.

And I never got myself a nickname. And I didn't do any military service, so just call me Philipp.

I will.

Where's your dog?

My dog?

I've seen you with a black dog a couple of times.

He's, that is, she's a girl, I said. At the moment, she's . . . *with my boyfriend* would have been the right answer, but I said: on vacation.

On vacation, he repeated.

On vacation, I repeated. I've got to go.

Thanks for not giving me any cigarettes, he called after me.

Philipp has taken the children to his mother's for vacation. She has just finished her first phase of chemotherapy. She's as bald as Buddha, not fat at all, though, of course not, she hasn't had any appetite for months and can't force herself to eat. She prefers wearing orange. It's full of life, she says, I like this color best. After she was diagnosed with breast cancer in the spring, she had an operation, then several rounds of chemotherapy, and finally radiation daily for several weeks. Every child needs a summer vacation, she says, and we even have a salt-water open-air swimming pool here, it's like being on the seashore. The children swallow the salt water and take turns getting a fever. The children are homesick. Philipp calls and asks: Who wants to talk to Mama? The big little one talks about a crocodile in his bed. The little little one says: Mama, Grandma, ice cream. Philipp takes the phone from him and tells me that he was standing at her door, ringing the bell. When she didn't answer, the big little one got completely worked up and Philipp had thought she'd "fallen asleep." He added: You know what I mean.

The dog is stretched out under my desk. She has a white face and is sleeping, her mouth open slightly. Her tongue dangles out lifelessly. She twitches, I breathed a sigh of relief. This summer, for the first time, I had her sheared like a sheep. She accepted it without reacting. Her wool fell thickly from both sides, and she climbed from the waves as if peeled, then bounded away, looking years younger. How sweet, people say when I walk her around the block, the same people who'd never paid us any attention. What kind of dog is that? they ask. It looks like a fox, they say. Yes, I answer, it's a black fox. They look at me, astonished, and I say: half. But foxes are red, Mama, everyone knows that, the big little one says on the phone when I tell him about it.

I sat in the darkened loge again and again. What I liked most was watching a set-change I was already familiar with. From *Othello* to *Mephisto,* for example. There were surprisingly many ways to change the stage set from one play to another. After a while, I knew everyone in the crew in silhouette and it wasn't lost on me that every shift was composed differently. If Philipp wasn't there, I left immediately. If he was there, I watched every movement of his hands, every one of his glances, the way he moved, his steps upstage and down. He was nimble, agile, and always moved unexpectedly. A black cat. I watched him, followed his every move, tried to predict his next step, got it wrong, guessed again, still wrong. I noted who he stood next to and who he spoke with, who he watched especially closely or often, who he joked around with, whose shoulder or head he patted. When he was too quiet for any length of time, someone always shouted: Philipp, what's up, everything OK? He'd crack a joke and everyone would laugh. For a few days, he seemed worn out. Sick or unhappy? That was the question I couldn't answer by looking at him. He seemed listless, lethargic, seemed to creep rather than walk, and didn't speak to anyone. It lasted only a few days, then it was over, and afterward seemed unreal, even hard to imagine.

He says the seven-year itch is over. Three days before he left with the children, it was our anniversary. I didn't get back from a meeting until late. My flight was delayed. I sat around in the Basel Mulhouse airport, the *EuroAirport,* for four hours. I couldn't even read. I was annoyed. I kept asking myself why on earth I'd agreed to go to the meeting, which was, of course, as always, so important it was absolutely impossible to reschedule. Go ahead, Philipp had said. It's enough if you're home in the evening. When I called to tell him about the delay, he said: Maybe you won't be that late after all; try to think positively for once at least. I'll have the babysitter come in any case. As we approached for landing, I wanted to rip off my seatbelt, jump up, run to the door, kick it down, and jump out of the plane. After we landed, I could barely get out of my seat. I slunk to the exit, through the gangway, the terminal, the arrivals hall. I wanted to take a taxi, but that wouldn't have brought the evening back either. So I sat in the train, changed twice, and walked the last bit. The tears welled up as I climbed the stairs. By the time I put my key in the lock, it was after eleven. I'm sorry, I said. He kissed away a tear. Come on, everything's fine.

The nicest thing about the loge was the plush upholstered chair, which I could place as needed to watch Philipp on whichever part of the stage he was working. I took off my shoes and rested my legs on the railing and occasionally fell asleep by the end of the set change. Once the caretaker came to check the light bulbs. He was startled when I said: Don't be startled. I'm going to have to report this, he teased. I didn't sit there again.

I avoided Philipp. If I saw him at the entrance, I'd wait until he was gone. If he was sitting in the cafeteria, I'd turn on my heel. If he was heading my way in the labyrinth of passages below stage, I'd swerve away. Once, he appeared so suddenly right in front of me, I couldn't escape. He said: My sister read your book. I didn't dare ask what she thought of it. I said: It's my first book. I know, he answered. And repeated: My sister read it. And that was a lie, it now occurs to me, that we never spoke about. Now it's too late. He'd deny it all, as usual.

In May, summer abruptly followed a cool, windy spring. One of our productions was invited to Vienna. I left my dog with Jakob in Bonn, as I always did when I couldn't take care of her myself, drove back to Hamburg, and missed my flight. On arriving in Vienna I went straight to the theater. Philipp stood in front of me at the stage entrance.

Did you have a nice trip?

I can't say that. I missed my flight.

I know, it caused a big commotion, but now you're here, so relax.

Who was so worked up?

Everyone! The people in Hamburg, those in Vienna, the director, the dramaturge, the theater management, everyone.

I had no idea you were here, too.

Well, I am. Come, they're waiting for you.

He moved silently, agile, lithe, a black cat. It, no, *he* led me through countless doors and hallways, left, left again, right, down several flights of stairs, back up and straight ahead, until he stopped in front of an iron door.

Good luck.

I could use it.

I'll keep watch.

For what?

To make sure nothing happens.

After the Vienna premiere there was a party, fittingly, after which the last ones to leave went to a bar, as they always do, and at some point afterward I ended up in a taxi with him.

When we appeared at breakfast, someone asked in a concerned tone: Did something happen to you?

Yes, Philipp replied.

You two look like you were in an accident.

We were, Philipp said, we ran into a couple of angels.

We spent four more days in Vienna, played four more shows in the evenings, stayed up four more nights alternately in his hotel room or in mine. Then it was time for my flight home. Philipp had to stay for two more days to break down the set. I suffered through violent and protracted pains in my side that I attributed alternately to my stomach, my kidneys, and my liver.

I miss the children. I call Philipp's mother. What did you think? she asks, in this heat they're in the outdoor pool. Philipp's got nerves of steel, you know. He lets them run around, jump in the pool, dive under water, I can't bear to watch.

How are you doing?

Oh I'm fine, really.

Is the chemo tough on you?

No, though I have to say, I am happy the little ones are here.

Are you sure it's not too much for you? You've got to take care of yourself.

No, everything's perfect.

That's his mother. She's always doing well. There's no problem, never has been. Every storm will pass, you know. When her husband gambled away his own restaurant business, she found herself a job and one for him, too. No problem, everyone's got to work, she says. When alcohol destroyed his liver so badly he could no longer work, he stayed at home resting while she worked double shifts as a cook. When she found him in their oldest daughter's bed one day, she quickly shut the door again. Their daughter left the house soon anyway, she'd had her heart set on becoming a teacher. When her husband died, she passed up the inheritance, no problem, and started all over again, moved into a small apartment with Philipp, there was less to clean that way, signed the younger daughter up for an apprenticeship in a hotel, met some men. Eventually, when none of the men stayed around, it was wonderful, she had her peace and quiet. When Philipp got into trouble at school, trouble with the authorities, trouble with the police: It will all work out, things are never as bad as they seem. When the older daughter had a breakdown and was admitted to a psychiatric clinic: That's good, she'll get some rest and will make her peace with the world. That's important, you know, she says, things never stay the way they are.

Of course she'd noticed the lump in her breast, she says, but she didn't worry about it, that's how it is, it will go away again. When the doctor was auscultating her lungs because of a stubborn cold, his stethoscope bumped against the tumor the size of an egg in her breast. Good lord, he said. Oh, I've had that for a long time, she said.

When do you think they'll be back from the pool?

It's hard to get the little ones out of the water, she replied.

I'll try again in the evening, I say, enjoy the peace and quiet. I open the balcony door, the dog curls up under my desk, I close the door. I check how hot it is outside online. The current weather conditions in Hamburg, I can even narrow it down to a particular neighborhood, ninety-three degrees. The dog shakes her head, and I say: We'll stay indoors. I brush the dog. It, that is, *she* twitches, the wire brush tickles the skin under her close shorn fur.

Where's your dog? he asks.

My dog?

Is he away on vacation again?

What do you mean, on vacation?

Well, he's not here in any case, Philipp said when he finally came to my place, forty-nine hours later, straight from the airport.

She's in Bonn.

What's in Bonn?

My boyfriend.

Silence.

And what do we do now?

I'll call Bonn now.

Good, I'll go out, I'll . . . go have a beer in the place on the corner.

Jakob, who learned right then that he was my ex-boyfriend, kept the dog. She's staying here, he said. When you've worked through whatever this is, get in touch. He hung up.

I called him again but got the answering machine. She's not a bargaining chip, I said and hung up before starting to cry.

But that's exactly what she was, as he assured me the following day. He refused to hand her over. I would see her again only after I dropped that idiot and came back to him.

The next day—we'd been a couple for a week—we decided to get married. All my life, I'd ruled out marriage for me. If I remember correctly, I said to Philipp: You know, we could get married. And he replied: Good idea. A few hours later, I said: That was a stupid idea. And he replied: I don't think it is. We drove to the civil registry office the next morning. We'd expected to walk out as husband and wife, but it doesn't work that quickly, the official lectured us, and that's a good thing. We could register with her office to get married but would only get an appointed date and time once my native parish had issued a Certificate of No Impediment, and that, she estimated, would take a month.

She was right to the day. So we had four weeks to order wedding rings and get to know each other a bit.

Just so I know—after all, I'm about to take your name—were your ancestors Nazis? I asked early in the third week.

Weren't all Germans Nazis? Philipp asked in response.

That's a good question and an easy answer. About your own family, I'd like a bit more information.

And your proper Swiss family, how much Nazi gold is there in your cellar? He wagged his right foot impatiently.

I laughed. In this case, my poverty is my moral wealth, I replied. Philipp scowled at me. Am I imagining it or is your tone downright self-righteous?

Come on, Philipp, were your relatives members of the Nazi Party? Or in one of their sub-organizations—what do I know, the

Hitler Youth or the German Students' League? Or in the National Socialist People's Welfare? Or the German Labor Front?

I don't believe so, he said. There is one uncle, maybe he was. A few years ago, on his ninetieth birthday, he called out *Sieg Heil!* He was already senile and no longer knew what time he was living in.

You mean he thought it was nineteen-forty and celebrating his thirtieth birthday?

Philipp looked at me uncertainly. Probably, he said softly. His answer sounded more like a question.

It's simply not getting dark. It's not cooling off at all. I'm waiting for dusk to walk the dog. She's stretched out under my desk. When she's lying somewhere else, on the tiles in the bathroom or in the kitchen, I can't write. Come, come on back here, I say, lie down near me. She sighs, she obeys. Or sometimes not. When she doesn't, I want to push her under the desk and make her lie down. I try to do it with words. I'm writing a love story, I tell her, lie down near me, come here, my sweetheart. She doesn't move. I can't think of anything to write without you, so come here and work with me! She gets up, stretches her front legs, yawns, shakes herself, and trots into my office.

At ten-thirty we go out, evening is falling. I'm wrapped up in my story. We walk along the canal. A light sways toward us, ding-a-ling, the elderly woman on the bicycle calls out and yanks her handlebars to steer away at the last moment. Old idiot, I shake my head and keep walking. The dog is gone. I spin around in a circle, she's gone. I stand still and listen. Something prevents me from calling her name. I think things over. Nothing. A terrible presentiment washes over me. I climb over the railing and stumble down the embankment. You goddamn mongrel, I swear, trying to chase away the dread, when I get my hands on you, I'm going to break your neck. Nothing. Grabbing tree roots, I scramble back up the embankment. She's kept me company for ten years and now she's gone. I sit on the railing. My mind is empty. Now I'll go home, unlock the door, sit down at my desk, and finish the chapter. I look at the ground. My dog is sitting next to me. Have you completely lost your mind, why did you scare me like that? She smiles.

A few weeks later but before the Certificate of No Impediment arrived, the doorbell rang. Jakob, with my dog. You're the one who should be taking care of it, he tells me, after all it's your dog. And get in touch when you've calmed down.

Calmed down?

Yes, calmed down.

How are you doing?

Things are good. I'm doing a lot of shoots. Dogs aren't allowed on the set.

She was back. At first I wept with joy, then with emotion. Philipp looked at her with interest for a while, but also skeptically. She looked at him the same way. I introduced the two of them, then had to go to the toilet urgently. When I came back, they were facing each other in exactly the same way. They were sizing each other up. Cat and dog, both of them black.

Philipp learned quickly. Even before our wedding day, passersby assumed the dog was his. They also look alike. With their thick black hair, people would say, it's often that way with dogs and their owners, similar appearances. In fact, they can't stand each other. Their natures are incompatible. But I'm attached to this dog, we live together, work together, are silent together. Most of the time, even if I just clear my throat, she understands. For ten years. She was first.

I take down the laundry I'd hung up in the afternoon. Heat fills the attic drying room. The roof beams creak. Only men's clothing: huge, little, tiny. And one pair of my underwear, that's it. I make three piles. Big one, big little one, little little one, I murmur alternately. Philipp's clothes are heavy. The children's clothes seem absurdly small. They can't possibly fit in them! Big little one, little little one, now and again I can't decide. Does the big one still wear this or does the little one now? The little one wears what the big one wore. When I hold the smallest clothes and try to picture the boys wearing them, I can't do it. I can only see the little little one, the older images are gone. I go downstairs, look at photographs, and lose track of time.

Monday, July 3, at 11:20. No one wants to get married then, the opening is still available. It was a bright, beautiful morning. We put on some nice clothes, took the small box with the rings, tied a flower on the dog, hoped both marriage witnesses would be on time, and took a taxi to the registry office. The registrar recited a love poem by Erich Fried in a pompous, solemn, sluggish tempo, and the fact that she knew it by heart made it more embarrassing. It's nonsense says reason, it's calamity says calculation, it's nothing but pain says fear, it's hopeless says insight, it's ridiculous says pride, it's foolish says caution, it's impossible says experience, it is what it is says love. This poem is apparently as much a part of the procedure as the question do we want to get married, but in the end, the tears did come, and the registrar smiled and handed me a tissue so quickly she must have had it at the ready. When we came out of the registry office, through the backdoor, like all newlyweds, Philipp's colleagues, whom I recognized from a distance, showered us with rice. We went down to the Elbe, sat at a café, drank champagne, were happy, and went swimming. The dog sprayed us with water from her coat.

Philipp can climb steep walls and confidently make his way, cat-like, along the narrowest of walkways and edges. From the loge, I once watched him break down the set from a play not worth mentioning while I was going over my lines for a similar play to be performed that evening. Philipp was standing on some kind of half-pipe, an oversized U made of chipboard, unscrewing bolts, which he then handed to a colleague standing next to him. From below, someone busy in the arc of the U called out: Philipp, what's up, things OK? And, without looking up or interrupting his work, Philipp started to warble something I couldn't hear in a thin, high voice. He seemed to be imitating someone his colleagues all recognized, and they laughed; because of the falsetto voice, I thought it must be a woman and it caught my attention. I put down my script and listened attentively without understanding any of it. Philipp's colleagues looked up at him and doubled over with laughter. The one next to him, holding the screws, bent over, laughing so hard that he tipped over and fell. Afterward, I couldn't explain how it happened: Philipp caught him and pulled him back up, stood him on the edge, and calmed him down. Their colleagues were speechless. After a moment, Philipp started warbling into the silence again and everyone, even the one who'd just narrowly missed falling five meters to the stage below, burst into more laughter. Their relief seemed to fan their hilarity, they shook, they heaved, they writhed, they groaned, they were beside themselves.

Philipp's Uncle Günter and Aunt Sigrid wanted to meet their new niece. Over coffee on the terrace, they patiently explained, who was who in the family, one relative after another. I nodded, ate strawberry tart, and hoped the family wasn't too big. When they got to the *Sieg Heil* uncle, my ears perked up. Was he a Nazi? I asked. You are good, Aunt Sigrid said. He was a guard in Bergen-Belsen and after the camp was liberated by the British in April, 1945, he fled. The bite of strawberry tart fell off my fork, I looked at Philipp, who was sitting across from me, calmly eating his tart. The fugitive uncle was hidden, I learned, by three sisters who ran a restaurant on the Lüneberg Heath. They offered this stranger refuge in their attic. The oldest sister had two daughters, one of whom is Philipp's mother. The youngest one fell so completely in love with the fugitive camp guard that, after he was discovered and sentenced by a British military court to fifteen years, she swore she would wait for him. And she did. She was twenty-eight when her beloved was put in prison, she would be forty-three when he got out. Too old to start a family. Nevertheless, she waited for her convicted war criminal. In 1955, after serving ten years, he was pardoned, they married and had four children even though his wife was already thirty-eight years old. I looked at Philipp again: Why didn't you tell me this?

Oh, he probably didn't know, it's ancient history, his aunt answered for him. Philipp nodded. I'm not even related to that camp guard he told me later. He was a great-uncle by marriage. You've got to realize: my great-aunt, my mother's aunt married this guy.

But your grandmother, as the oldest of the three sisters, hid this war criminal. And your own mother spent her childhood and adolescence in this restaurant, where the atmosphere, to put it very mildly, was extremely sympathetic to the Nazis!

That's not her fault, Philipp said.

Yes, but why didn't you tell me?

I did tell you about my uncle and his Nazi salute on his ninetieth birthday. I don't understand why you're attacking me like this.

Philipp took me in his arms. No one had told him the uncle's story that clearly, he said. And he'd forgotten a lot, too, he found it all unspeakably repellent. He sniffed at my temples. On the other hand, he didn't find me repellent at all. He kissed my ear, it tickled. I turned away, he kissed my other ear. I let my head fall back, he kissed my collarbone—I gave up all resistance.

Mama, the big little one says, imagine, Grandma gave me a pig and it stinks, it's gross.

Can't you wash it?

No, it's too gross, it's always that way. You can't do anything about it.

And now?

Now I'm sniffing it. Ecwww, it's gross, yuck! Do you want to? I'd rather not.

Should the pig stay with Grandma?

Yes, leave it at Grandma's.

The little little one asks: Mama? Mama? Mama?

Yes, sweetheart.

Mama?

Yes, this is Mama.

Mama?

Yes, my love.

Mama?

Could you put Grandma on?

Grandma?

Yes, put her on.

Mama?

Yes!

Grandma!

Yes, that's right, put her on.

It's Philipp. She's sleeping, he says, anything wrong?

No.

What did you want to ask her?

Just how she's doing.

She's exhausted. Philipp is out of breath.

What's going on?

Oh nothing, he gasps for breath, it's just that she sleeps so much, she's always falling asleep.

Don't assume anything bad.

You're one to say that! I have to hang up, the kids are fighting again.

Philipp knew, because I told him before we were married, that I'd watched him from the darkened loge at work on the brightly lit stage for months. I told him about seeing the fall. He smiled. It wasn't as dramatic as my description, he said. I reminded him of the scene, described what happened step-by-step up to the moment when he reached into the emptiness, fast as lightning, and grabbed his colleague. Philipp nodded. You should never look down, that's all. Being Swiss and an experienced mountain climber, you must know that. The moment someone starts falling forward, you can't think: Oh God, he's falling, but instead: I've got him. The idea becomes fact. First you have the image, then it becomes reality. Like in the theater. First the model, then the staging. That all sounds good, I said, and that one time, it all worked wonderfully, but it's not a workable model to just close your eyes and believe that will make everything terrible vanish from the world.

There are things that are too terrible to look at closely, Philipp replied. When you learn as a ten-year-old, that your nice uncle who used to live in the attic, actually comes from hell, where he worked as a satanic overseer to make sure the horror lasted, that it escalated, that the mountains of corpses lying on the bare ground got higher, that the countless prisoners in all stages of emaciation, that the thousands of terminally ill, starving, skeletal people in their contaminated barracks did not recover—when you learn this as a ten-year-old, you have to look away, you can't look into that abyss or you'll fall into it.

Before his mother's tumor was removed from her breast, I took her to the hospital for a pre-op examination. I invited her to lunch, lentil stew and with it a small beer because I encouraged her to order one. She took the first sip, had a white foam moustache and said: Wonderful. Isn't it wonderful? And how nice that we have time to chat. I asked her if she was afraid. Nooo, she said sounding stubborn, if I let terrible things get to me, I'd have passed away long ago. She put down her beer glass without noticing the rumpled napkin under it. The glass fell over.

How's the mutt? Philipp constantly makes unfriendly remarks about the dog or reminds me that the lifespan of a dog this size, and because she's a mixed breed, the lifespans of the two particular breeds is (apparently) twelve years. Two more years, he sighs as he vacuums up dog hair, removes a tick, or takes a shredded toy from her, two more years.

It's too hot for her, I reply, but thanks for asking. I'm touched you're concerned about the dog.

Silence.

Philipp, why did you call?

The children are asleep. I just wanted to say good night.

Good night.

And to ask if you miss us.

Philipp . . . Isn't it dangerous for you to take both boys alone to the pool?

You just don't trust me, that's the problem, he says.

Yes, that is the problem.

Should I hang up?

Do you want to?

Silence.

And are you able to work?

Yes. I'm writing a love story, I say.

That's nice, he says.

You're in it.

You're not serious.

I am serious.

What are you writing about?

How we met.

That's really nice.

Yes, it was.

Should I hang up?

If you want to.

Nooo, he says sounding stubborn, nooo, I don't want to.

8

Key player

He came into the classroom last, stopped in the middle of the room, opened his eyes wide and looked me over from bottom to top and back down. Then he grinned. A strikingly tall, strikingly thin, strikingly good-looking, young black man in a baseball hat.

Bonjour, Madame, he says.

I scrutinize the list. Name?

Mathieu ninety-six, he says. Simple, right?

What's the ninety-six?

The year I was born.

What?

The knocking starts. - / * * / - - / * . I thought I was done with this. I hadn't heard any knocking all spring. Over the summer, there were a few short, sharp attacks in monotonous staccato, not worth deciphering, and now this a second time and distinct: long / short short / long long / short : TIME. And again, a third time. I pressed my fingertips against my temples.

He looked at me with sympathy. Is everything OK, Madame?

I nod and try to smile.

The students are supposed to bring their chairs into a circle. There are some collisions, metal chair legs clinking against each other; watch out! No, you watch out! One of them knocks his chair over, another trips over it. Both are immediately ready to fight. Sit down, the teacher calls, clapping her hands, sit down now.

I'd gotten a list of the students' names from the office, but they were all made up names: Crystal Flower, Snoopy, Warrior Mouse. I show the teacher. Those are their usernames to log into the computer, she says. She tries to match them to the students, gives up, and hands the list back to me.

Would you start, please? I ask the good-looking, young, black man formally, what's your name? Screams of laughter, as if someone had flipped a switch. We don't address the students formally here, the teacher says. This is Mathieu. *Mathieu?* You've shown up at just the right time. What a coincidence. The knocking starts again. - * - * / * * * */ * * / * - * * / - * * ? That was too fast. Silence.

In 1996 I was pregnant. It seems like just yesterday. Now I'm standing in front of twenty-three young adults who were born that year. After the *procedure* I found some baby shoes at a flea market, put them in my bag, and ran away. Mathieu has enormous feet. What size shoe do you wear?

I like you, Madame, he says, forty-seven, why?

I like you, too, Mathieu, I think to myself. You're handsome. You're charming. You don't mind looking ridiculous. You're gutsy. You're seventeen, and you're checking me out.

I'm here to write a book with you. A book? Crystal Flower asks. It would be more of a brochure than a book, the organizers had assured me when I asked the same question as incredulously as Crystal Flower is asking now. I nod and say: Yes, a book. She looks at me, horrified. What for? I put her question to the group. Does anyone have an idea? Mathieu is the only one to raise his hand. It would have been enough just to nod at him, but I say: Yes, Mathieu. I have a question, Madame, he leans forward, elbows on his thighs, will this book sell?

Of course, I reply.

Great, he says, and who gets the profit? Us, I hope.

You're an enterprising author, that's good, I say. That's something most writers have to learn how to be.

Buying and selling, Madame, no one's going to pull one over on me.

The fact is, Mathieu, I say as I think about his comment, that this project has initial costs, paper and printing, but also labor costs.

Are you paid to come here, Madame? he asks.

That's the reason I'm here, I reply.

Hunh, says the one who calls himself Oreo, and I have to laugh.

I wrote up a questionnaire. I put the questions to the group. With whom should I begin? No one offers. Mathieu?

Yes, Madame?

Should I start with you?

If you'd like.

Good. First question: Do you believe in love?

Yes.

He says it as if he were confirming his name. Yes, period.

Next question, he says.

Now it's your neighbor's turn. The second question is for you, Oreo—you're name is Derric, right? He remains expressionless.

Derric, do you believe in God?

Partly.

The next question is for Big Bang—the teacher shrugs. Abdul, Big Bang says. Thank you, Abdul. Tell me, do we live in a just country?

Abdul thinks this over. There are worse countries. He shakes his head. He thinks it over some more. So-so, he says.

Warrior Mouse, who's that? The teacher whispers to me. Jennifer? She gives me a hostile look. She's one of the two who were ready to go at each other earlier. I skip one question and ask her: Jennifer, have you ever been in a fight? Peals of laughter.

Yes, Jennifer answers, and I've even been knocked out.

Next question. Tayfun. That's his real name, the teacher says. Good. Tayfun, are the police your friends and helpers?

No, he replies, anything else!

I work my way around the circle with my questions. Whenever

possible, the students answer with just yes or no. Most of them answer very quickly, as if to show they're not even listening.

Next to last question: Gloria, are there any modern heroes?

No, Gloria says.

I ask the question again, she repeats her answer. I ask the whole group: modern heroes? They shake their heads.

Last question—hang on, how did I end up with you again, Mathieu? Did I miss anyone?

Büşra's not here today, Nesrin, the crystal flower, calls out.

I'm happy to answer another question, Madame, Mathieu says. Knocking. Long short long short / short short short short / short short / short long short short / long short short. Mathieu looks at me expectantly.

If you had the power, what would you outlaw?

Without hesitation he says: cyber-bullying, discrimination, racism, despotism. He smiles at me. That was easy, he says.

I still have the baby shoes. I'd forgotten about them. I didn't think of them when I gave birth to my sons two and four years ago. Nor when my sons were learning to walk and I bought them their first shoes. I keep them in the big black chest we used when we went on summer vacation, my parents, my brothers, and I. It still has a label with my dead father's name and the address of my parents' house, where I'd found it in the attic. The shoes are made of blue leather. The shoelaces, stitching, and soles are blindingly white. They've never been worn. I hadn't noticed this back then when I saw them in the Vienna flea market and grabbed them. That *rag market,* as the Viennese call it, sold second-hand things. I can still remember the musty smell of that Sunday morning in autumn on the Danube Canal when I let myself drift with the tide of people rummaging through the stalls when my eyes fell on the pair of tiny shoes, *for my son.* I took them and hurried away.

The teacher is waiting for me outside the classroom and apologizes for the fact that seven of the students are absent. She called each of them during the free period, but she has to admit, it's very hard to keep hold of her clientele. There's no consistency, in either their attendance or performance.

You shouldn't take it personally when your students skip class, I tell her and she gives me an irritated look. She holds the door open for me. Mathieu is not there. I look around. He's not there! The teacher watches me. I slowly take out my notes. Why is Mathieu not here? I read out the list of nicknames, they answer with *here* or *absent*. Anyone know why? I ask each time I hear *absent*. For Mathieu96, the warrior mouse Jennifer answers: He's sick. I want to ask how she knows but assume the teacher will think I'm going too far. She's standing right next to me. You shouldn't take it personally, she says softly and smiles. The homework topic was *What makes me really furious*. I make my way down the rows and collect their work. Most of the students, and this puzzles me, have added exactly the same phrase: I don't want you to read this to the class.

If I don't name any names, may I read your work out loud? I ask.

They hesitate. I'd rather you didn't, Snoopy says, everyone will recognize me anyway. I look for Snoopy's homework and read it through:

I get furious when I realize that people are talking about me behind my back and don't have the guts to talk to me directly. And when some chick flirts with my friend (and makes a pass at him)! Or when I don't have any cigarettes or when someone stupidly comes on to me without making it clear.

Okay, Snoopy, I'll keep it to myself. But part of writing, I tell them, is the desire to be indiscreet. Your next assignment is: *A secret I have always wanted to tell.* Naturally you can also tell secrets that aren't yours, which may make it easier. All right, get started!

I gather the papers at the end of the period. The teacher promises to get the assignment from the seven who are absent. A deadline is essential, she says, the shorter, the better.

Then let's say by ten PM tonight.

It's best to communicate with the students on Facebook, it's a medium with positive associations, one the students trust.

Was that a joke? A teachers' inside joke? Apparently not since she asks: You do have a Facebook page, I hope? I nod and she looks relieved. That's good. I'll tell the students they should write you directly and send a friend request, OK?

I hesitate.

Naturally you can unfriend them when the project is finished.

It's quarter past nine. My husband is working the night shift as he has almost every night lately. I'm alone with the sleeping children and the sleeping dog. Under my desk, she twitches in her dream. I sit down and read the sixteen secrets that had wanted to be told. The sixteen that I collected at the end of class.

From Jennifer Heitmann. I saw my friend's father in the train station with a strange woman, but I can't tell my friend. If her mother finds out, she'll kill him. Or herself.

From Nesrin Gül. I know that my friend doesn't go to her tutoring sessions on Tuesdays and Thursdays, but meets her German boyfriend who she loves more than anything else.

From Marvin Gosch. I have a friend whose father has a new family. Now he pays his old family less support so they'll get welfare. But the son can't work after school anymore or the welfare checks will be cut. That father should be reported to the authorities, he's ruining his son's life.

Always about friends . . . and yet the first word is always *I*. I glance at the clock: a few minutes before ten. I look at my Facebook page. There are two messages. Nothing from Mathieu. I make myself a cup of coffee. The clock strikes ten. I see that Mathieu is online. I can't help it, I write him.

Are you thinking about the assignment, Mathieu?

He answers right away: Don't panic, almost done.

My coffee's finished, but nothing has come. It's already ten-thirty. Horrible brat. I decide to go to bed. A new message.

Good evening, Madame, here's my secret. My father is an Evangelical-Presbyterian pastor. If he finds out I have a girlfriend (atheist), he will disown me. With best wishes, Mathieu.

I shut down the computer.

We'd chosen a name for the fun of it. If we have a child, we'll call it Paul, Jakob said.

Even if it's a girl?

Jakob laughed. If it's a girl? There are no girls in my family.

And why did you choose Paul?

It's a nice name, Jakob answered, and it rhymes with bawl.

I shook my head. Let me read, Jakob, please.

Yes, you need your peace and quiet. You yourself said you can't stand screaming children, that's why I chose Paul. Paul, don't bawl.

You're crazy, Jakob.

No, you're crazy, with your neurotic need for quiet. If someone's got a pulse, he bothers you, whether his name is Jakob or Paul. Think about that. I'm going for a walk, that way you'll have some peace and quiet.

Freshly fallen wet leaves cover the bike path. I'm late and can't ride as fast as I'd like. Behind the main train station the underpass is being repaired and is closed off. Heavy traffic. I swerve onto the street abruptly and a car shoots by me so close that my handlebars shake. I brake. My front tire veers, I fall. A van honks, swerves around me, soaks me with spray. My leg hurts. I pick up my bicycle, swing into the saddle, and push on the pedal as if I were in a race.

The bicycle stands in front of the school are empty. As I'm locking my bike, Tayfun runs up to me. I'm lucky. You're late, too. He's breathing so hard, he can hardly speak. You're all wet.

I know.

And dirty. The back of your coat is completely black. Do you want to go into class like that?

I don't have any choice.

Good morning, sorry I'm late, let's get started right away. I've read the *secrets you've always wanted to tell*, put them together, and made them into one long text. We're going to read it together now.

The students stare at me. Only Mathieu is studying his pencil closely.

I give the class a friendly nod. So, who would like to read?

I hear Tayfun whisper: She came by bike. Giggles.

Exactly, I say, I rode here on my bicycle, like I always do. If you have any questions about that, I'll be happy to answer them after class.

Silence.

Mathieu, please.

Please what?

Please read out loud.

No thank you. He keeps studying his pencil.

The teacher steps in. Mathieu, would you please read?

No, I'd rather not, he replies and bends down to get his bag from under the desk. He opens it and tosses his pencil in. He straightens up. We wait. I look at him impassively. Finally, he picks up the sheet of paper, looks at it contemptuously and starts to read—haltingly—in a soft voice, as vulnerable as a small child learning to speak. Every time he pauses, the other students help him with the next word, the next phrase, the next sentence. He repeats after them, he stretches some words out, shortens others, he mumbles and coughs through others. If I didn't have the text in front of me, I couldn't have understood him.

At the passage with the pastor father and the atheist girlfriend, everyone laughs, even Mathieu. His confidence is restored.

So, what's your girlfriend's name? Derric calls.

Latoya, Mathieu answers, pursing his lips and blowing a kiss.

Latoya, a few of them scream. Mathieu makes a calming gesture. Guys, stay cool, always. And to me: Is that enough, or do I have to keep reading?

He comes up to me after class. What's up, Mathieu? I ask casually and pack up my notes.

You said we could ask now. Your pants look bad, here, on the side, look.

Thanks, I know. I fell.

You fell? He opens his eyes wide, like he did when we first met. He looks me up and down. He nods. You were lucky, Madame, very lucky.

I pick up my bag and go to the door. He follows. I can't find the light switch.

Here, Madame, you can turn them off here, he says, reaching past me.

Thank you, Mathieu.

I walk down the long hallway to the front entrance, Mathieu at my side.

And you, why don't you tell a secret, too? he suddenly asks.

I'm so surprised, I stop walking. A secret?

Do you have a boyfriend?

No, I'm married.

Maybe you have a boyfriend anyway?

Mathieu, that's enough. See you next week, goodbye. I walk away. After a few steps I turn back. He's gone. The hallway is empty except for Jennifer, the warrior mouse, who is standing next to the yucca plant, watching me. I wave at her. She turns away.

Mathieu is almost two heads taller than I am. Most boys these days are so tall. Jakob, Paul's father, is 5'11" if I remember correctly, almost short by today's standards. And Paul, how tall would he have been? Would he have towered over me like Mathieu? If Paul put his arm around my shoulder and I looked up, what would I see? An enormous, pointy Adam's apple, follicles inflamed from shaving, acne? I put the blue baby shoes on my desk. Size 19 is stamped in the shaft. Forty-seven minus nineteen equals twenty-eight. There are twenty-eight sizes between these blue shoes and the sneakers Mathieu wears. That would make a six-yard long, double row of twenty pairs of shoes, as long as the hallway from the kitchen to my office. Knocking. Now I recognize it: CHILD.

I got a message from Mathieu. Madame, you forgot to give us an assignment. But I'm asking for your consideration. I have two important games this week.

Consideration?! Excellent word choice. I look at the clock. Philipp is picking up the children for once, so I have time. I write back: Mathieu, you're absolutely right. Thanks for reminding me. Here is a special (very considerate) assignment for you: What should our book be about? By 10 PM tonight.

P.S. What do you play?

A minute later, at 4:13, Mathieu's answer comes.

I play basketball, Madame. The story should be about love and violence. About shady dealings, possibly. Betrayal wouldn't be bad. And there should be some sex (a little), so the book will sell.

(4:14): Mathieu, can you think of a worthy protagonist?

(4:14): What's that?

(4:15): A main character.

(4:18): A man, then. I see him as eighteen years old, a drug dealer. He earns money on the side from illegal cage fights. He dreams of being a famous rap star. He comes from Mexico. I'll call him Kalim. He's ruthless and a racist.

(4:20): That's good, Mathieu. Good luck in your games.

(4:25): Thanks, Madame, I will be lucky.

I click on Mathieu's profile and look at his friends. At seventeen, he has 377 friends. I don't see a Latoya.

I'd always liked Jakob's profile. He looks much more tender in profile than from the front. Forehead, nose, cheeks, chin: a perfectly composed hilly landscape. When Jakob noticed that I was looking at him from the side, he would look at me from the corner of his eye, without turning his head until I was afraid his eyeball would pop out and yelled look out! Paul would have inherited his profile, but with my dark eyes, my red mouth, and my small ears.

However, his hair would have come from Jakob, thick, honey-colored, wavy. And his long, thin hands and feet. And his strong eyebrows. And—I look for a photograph of Jakob and pin it on the wall in my office above my computer. What did you do that for? my husband asks when he comes home with the children. I'm trying to imagine what my son would look like, I reply, he'd be seventeen now.

Philipp looks at me. If I can help, I'll be in the next room. He leaves and shuts the door behind him. I take the photograph down and throw it in the desk drawer.

Today we want to start sketching out our story, I say and look up because a cell phone is ringing. Jennifer, please turn that off. The warrior mouse looks at me with hatred. But it's urgent, she says, I have to answer. Hello? She stands up and goes to the door. Yeah, hang on, she says, wait! The teacher runs after her, holds her back, tries to take the phone away. Jennifer throws it at her feet. Now we're going to the principal's office, the teacher says. Jennifer bursts into tears. No! You know what'll happen.

Jennifer has been given a final *last chance.* She sniffles into a tissue. Her telephone is on the lectern in front of me. The teacher had put it there, but not turned it off. On the screen, there's a picture of a cheerleader squad in a pyramid, in their blue sequined sweaters.

All right, let's take it from the top. We're now going to begin inventing the story. We have a few starting points: We've got a young man, Kalim. He's eighteen and he came from Mexico City to Hamburg five years ago. He dropped out of school and is a dealer. It's Sunday night, just after eleven. Kalim is sitting near the escalator in the square in front of the train station, waiting. For what? Or for whom? Invent a character who has something to do with Kalim. Who is this person, where does he or she come from, what does this character have to do with Kalim. You have a half-hour.

Madame! Mathieu raises his hand, already talking. Madame, you forgot the Kalim is also a rapper and an MMA master.

How do you know that? Abdul shouts.

It's simple, guys, Mathieu says, pointing at himself proudly several times, I invented Kalim.

They all look at me. Is that true? I nod. So if you have any questions about Kalim, ask Mathieu, his imaginative father. By the way, Mathieu, what's MMA?

Mixed martial arts, Madame, it's a kind of martial arts with very few restrictions or rules, extremely brutal. Kicking, hitting, grabbing, throwing, they're all allowed to defeat your opponent. And guys—Mathieu looks around the class—Kalim isn't just anyone. He earns money as a cage fighter, got it? If he weren't such a racist, we'd probably be friends. Mathieu leans back and crosses his arms. So, come up with something good. Something pretty, too, that'd be nice. He laughs.

Still sniffling, Jennifer lowers her head and starts writing. After ten minutes, she comes up to the front of the classroom, throws the crumpled tissue into the trashcan, and puts a sheet of paper on my desk. Done. Can I have my phone back?

What's this picture? I ask and point at the screen.

None of your business.

True. But I'm curious, it's my job to be curious. Are you a cheerleader?

I don't want you to write about me.

I promise.

That's my squad. The Angels.

Who are you cheering for?

The Blue Devils.

I glance over at Mathieu. Could you please come up to my desk? Thanks, Jennifer, I'll read it at home. I give her back her phone. The teacher raises her eyebrows. Jennifer asks if she can go to the restroom. Of course, I say, even though the teacher is making signs at me. Mathieu ambles up to my desk. Madame?

How did your games go?

So so. He grins. Are you interested in basketball?

Did you lose?

What do you think? Won one, tied the other.

What is your team called?

We're the Devils. Guess what position I play.

The Blue Devils? Thanks, Mathieu, you can go back to your seat.

He ambles back to his desk, turns and says: Point guard, Madame. I'm the key player.

Love and violence; shady dealings, possibly; betrayal and sex (a little) runs through my mind as I cycle home. I invented Kalim, guys. Mathieu, the key player. We're the Devils. Are you interested in basketball, Madame? The trees are bare, the leaves have been raked up. How quickly both happened. At a red light, I look up at the sky. A flock of greylag geese flies over me in an arrow formation, honking hoarsely. Their beaks glow dark yellow. Be sure to come back safe and sound, don't let yourselves get picked off, I say. The pedestrian next to me, an older gentleman in a hat, comes a step closer. He puts his hand to his ear. Excuse me, I don't hear well, he says. I was just wishing you a lovely day, I say and ride on. Yes, it is a lovely day, he replies and the sentence echoes in my ear.

I ride to the park, sit on a bench, and from my bag I take the pages the students handed in. I leaf through them, looking for Jennifer's paper.

By Jennifer Heitmann. A girl stands on the platform. She is Janua. She was meant to be a boy called Januar, but something went wrong. Janua has known Kalim forever (since he came to Germany = five years). When things are hard for her (most of the time), she calls him up and gets some grass. Now she's on her way home from street-dance practice and has to change trains at the main station. All of a sudden she sees her father, arm-in-arm with another woman. She runs up to them, pushes the woman onto the tracks and hits her father. But then she sees the two of them board the next train and realizes it was only a dream. She feels faint. She calls Kalim, she needs something to calm her down. They meet near the top of the escalator. Kalim has had a crush on Janua for years, but she doesn't care. She's interested in someone else, but hasn't ever told anyone who it is. The end.

Next page. A collaboration.

By Büşra Demir and Nesrin Gül.

Any resemblance to living persons is purely coincidental!

Hi everyone, I'm Ludovic. I'm handsome and vain. My parents come from Togo. I play basketball and have a good body. My girlfriend's name is Latoya. But maybe I'm just making that up. Of course, I'm always convinced that all girls are in love with me. Though it is true in a few cases, but I won't name any names. The stupid racist, Kalim, I know by sight. I'd like to beat him up even though he's much stronger and more brutal than I am. I'm just waiting for a good opportunity.

I look at two girls. They could be in my class. They're standing indecisively in front of a park bench and can't bring themselves to sit down because it looks too dirty. One of them is on the phone and chewing on her cuticles. The other one is looking for split ends. A small, beige dog sits in her handbag and yawns. The girls make signs at each other, tapping their temples, rolling their eyes, laughing noiselessly. What was I like at that age? What was it like to be seventeen? I knew what was right. I had definite opinions about almost everything. I sometimes envy that today. I didn't believe in God, but had an absolute view of good and evil. I was fundamentally on the side of the victim, the weak, the underdog, and the oppressed. Violence in any form was to be rejected, always, and in every case. No one had the right to kill another, not under any circumstances, which included mothers and their unborn children, no matter how young. A few years later, I myself decided against my child—that was the terminology used by the doctors and counselors I had to speak with before I lay down. I didn't kill it, I just decided against it. I decided. At seventeen, I would have spit in my face for this, would have turned my back. At twenty-five, I saw no other way.

Mathieu writes: (11:48): I'd like to speak with you.

I can't believe my eyes. It's late, I'm tired, and Mathieu has written. I drain my wine glass in one gulp and go to bed. My husband comes home, goes straight to the living room, turns on the television. The gunshots, the squealing tires reach me through the covers. I lie awake. I have nothing to talk about with you, Mathieu.

At 4:14 I write: What's it about?

At 9:13 he writes back: My father insists that I finish school, but my uncle wants to take me on as an apprentice.

(9:15): Of course you have to graduate first.

(9:56): I have to explain it to you.

Mathieu lives in the east part of the city, I live in the west. I agree to meet him briefly in the center of the city in the afternoon. He suggests the escalator in front of the train station. Where Kalim always hangs out. Kalim, the dealer he invented.

It's two o'clock. From a distance, I see him standing near the railing, one leg bent. I wheel my bicycle across the station square. He raises his arm, waves, and comes toward me, saying hello with a smile and looking unsteady on his feet.

There's no bench in the entire square. They don't want any bums here, Mathieu says. We seat on the red, imitation leather bench in the ticket office. You need to take a number, says a friendly railroad employee. Mathieu stands up and pushes the button. The machine spits out a ticket, and the employee nods, satisfied.

How often do you practice? I ask to avoid any silence.

At least twice a week and there are tournaments.

I see you have your own cheerleading squad.

He sighs. Yes, unfortunately. He pulls a note from his jacket pocket and hands it to me. Go ahead, open it, it's from Jennifer.

Hate me, love me, yell at me, hit me, kiss me, whatever. But don't ignore me.

I fold the note up again.

Are you a couple? Or were you once?

Good God, no, Madame, honest.

OK Mathieu, you wanted to talk to me about your uncle?

Yes, he says and hesitates, as if he were reluctant to change the subject. My uncle is a businessman, a very good one. He says I shouldn't waste my time. He's not going to wait for me. Now or never, Mathieu, he told me. I'm already seventeen.

You should definitely get your diploma and then find yourself a proper apprenticeship.

What do you mean by *proper*?

Not an informal one in the family, but an official one through a trade school with references and all that.

I figured you would say that.

Mathieu, everyone would say that, absolutely everyone and you know that perfectly well. Why are you asking me, of all people?

Don't know. You seem nice.

And there it is, the silence that immediately becomes significant. So to say something, anything, before it's too late, I ask: Your father's a pastor?

Yes. And he wants me to be a pastor, too. It's a good path, he says, but it's not mine, it really isn't. He looks at my hands, clasped in my lap.

What kind of church? I ask and loosen my hands.

The Ewe Evangelical Presbyterian Church. Mathieu looks me in the eye. That's my people, the Ewe, from Togo, Madame.

Hello! the friendly railroad employee calls, Five-five-three, isn't that you? It's your turn!

Yes! We jump up and have to laugh. Then we run out of the ticket office without a word.

I bend down and unlock my bicycle. Mathieu stands behind me. Do you have to leave already?

Yes. I stand up.

Thanks for the advice, he says. I turn around, his mouth speeds toward me and plants a kiss on my cheek.

Mathieu, please don't.

Why not? It's normal for friends.

I'm not your friend. He looks me up and down like the first time we met. He gives me a stubborn look. The thing is I like you, he says softly.

And Latoya?

Oh, her. He laughs. I made her up, too. Do you think I have talent?

As a writer?

He nods.

Could be. But you wanted to become a businessman.

He shrugs. I climb onto my bicycle. Goodbye, Madame. I ride off. Do you speak French at home? I call after him. He looks around. Of course, Madame. He keeps walking. His feet are huge.

P.S. Mathieu is not insulted that Büşra and Nesrin have written him into our story as Ludovic, on the contrary. He also thinks it's fine that Janua, the street dancer, is in love with him. But he insists that he, of course, will *not* be in love with her.

I won't be part of that, he says.

But somehow you have to be motivated to beat up Kalim, who everyone knows is into Janua.

I'll think of something, Madame, don't worry. I'll take care of that racist. I'll kill him if I have to, with good reason, just wait. To get a break from it, finally.

Yes, as long as we do it with you, I mean that we write it with you, I'll be there. Just wanted to say.

With best regards, Mathieu.

9

Swimming and flying

I don't know how things will continue. Either in this book, or in my life. I'm secretly waiting for someone to stumble into my life again and write more of the story. Number nine of twelve. Soon winter will be here. It blows on me in the morning, when I drag my bicycle out of the cellar and carry it, groaning, up the stairs, when I breathlessly ask the dog, whose winter coat has grown in, where she'd like to walk, and when, getting no answer as always, I drop my head back and watch my breath rise into the air. Soon winter will be here. What else? What has love got planned? Love. As if you don't have enough problems, my grandmother would say, first bread, then love! I press my lips together. Philipp had given me a kiss in the morning. The first in more than half a year. But he avoided my eyes, kept his closed; his lips were raw and moist at the same time.

I climb onto my bike and ride down the sidewalk, up to the next driveway with the sunken curb. Someone yells, don't fall! and my heavy utility bike promptly falls over. I recognize the voice right away. Creditor Number 17, our neighbor two doors down. He offers his hand, pulls me upright, takes a look at my trousers. Then he picks up my bicycle, checks the brakes, makes sure the seat and handlebars are straight. Did I startle you?

I grab the handlebars without a word. He does not let go. Our hands almost touch. I'm in a hurry, I say, and push off. He blocks my way. I haven't seen a cent yet.

I follow the debt consultant's advice for such instances. I reply: Please talk to Philipp.

No, I'm talking to you, I've run out of patience, says the neighbor, who lent my husband exactly three thousand euros.

I stick to the debt counselor's advice, give an understanding nod, and say: You got the debt payment schedule. It says when you'll get your first installment.

The schedule says that I won't get anything for two years, the neighbor replies, but I need the money now. His voice cracks. Now, he repeats.

And then I say exactly what the debt counselor emphatically warned me never to say: Fine, I'll take care of it.

I ride off without saying goodbye. My dog runs after me. A few weeks earlier, when the neighbor first blocked my way and wanted to know when he was going to get his money back, I didn't fall off my bike, even though it would have suited the situation. I just stood there, waiting to suffer the expected stroke. What money? This man, the head of a small family, was not on the list of creditors. More debts? One more person Philipp owes money to?

Philipp turned pale when I confronted him. His hands shook. He said he'd completely forgotten that one. No, he hadn't gambled again. He raised his right hand and swore that it was an old debt, not a relapse. He simply must have repressed it, he didn't know how. Unpleasant things just slip away from Philipp. It took me seven years of marriage to understand that they just disappear for him, cease to exist. That's not reassuring.

A penguin flies overhead. A _____? Penguins can't fly. Not for fifty million years, they haven't. Besides, there are no penguins in this country. And yet: instead of watching the street, I look at the sky. It's gone. There's nothing up there, nothing flying by. I stop. I close my eyes and try to picture it. The stout, milky, shimmering body, the streamlined head, the narrow wings, black like its face and beak. I don't really know much about winged creatures. I used to watch Humboldt penguins in the zoo and saw them again on television recently. It looked exactly like them. Exactly? Hang on. Did it have that characteristic black breast-band? Maybe, maybe not. Perhaps not. So maybe it wasn't a penguin. Just a bird. We mostly saw that kind of bird on Heligoland. We, that is Philipp and I. Last year, early in the summer, when everything was still in complete confusion, happily chaotic; when we were still a couple, not just parental units with joint property and lost trust, we decided at the last minute to get a baby- and a dog-sitter and take the boat to Heligoland. The sea was calm. When we landed, we were greeted by earsplitting birdcalls.

We rented "a romantic room for new lovers," sight unseen. A disgusting hole without windows or a bathroom and with a sagging, stained, but thoroughly comfortable bed. It was evening before we went for a walk on the beach. We reached the *Lummenfelsen*, the cliffs thick with murre colonies. In the fading light, we could just make out an entire swarm of countless little bodies, plump as potatoes, hurtling down forty meters, black against the black rock face. Lured by their parents' heart-breaking cries, the flightless chicks, only a few weeks old, shuffled toward the cliff's edge until they tipped into the void and were swallowed into the depths. After a few minutes, it was too dark to see anymore, but the cries of the parent birds didn't stop.

And some kind of murre like that just flew over me? In late autumn? From Heligoland to Hamburg? Murres are marine birds that spend the winter on the open seas and don't fly very well. Their stubby wings are better suited to paddling than flying. Their penguin-like body shape is an expression of their having adapted to life at sea. No, the idea that it was a murre is not convincing. The only possibility is—?!

Don't fall, I call after the creature whose breast I hadn't looked at carefully. I notice my dog's puzzled look and I click my tongue since words fail me. She gives me a resigned nod. I push into the pedal. I trust my dog to follow me on the sidewalk. Instead of looking at the street, I search the sky, but don't see anything.

Empty, cold air. Wintery air. Now what? Neighbors become creditors. Penguins fly. There! There it is again!

It flies over the construction site, where a candy factory had stood until just a few days ago and now luxury apartments are being built, past the crane drill and excavators digging out the cellar, and disappears behind the neighboring building. Breastband? Yes or no? It was too fast, it's gone, with or without a band. Given that it's flightless, it flies astonishingly well. As well as it dives. And when it dives—I observed this often enough in the penguin house at the zoo—it looks like it's flying. Its wings slide effortlessly and elegantly up and down. You can only tell that it's moving underwater and not in the air because of the swarms of fish it's chasing.

I dismount and look up. Where are you? The construction crane sways silently above me. I cower from its shadow.

Our rent is tied to the "local reference rent level." It increases with every renovation, with every new luxury building added to the neighborhood, with every euro more that a new neighbor (and the place is crawling with new neighbors) is willing to pay. Like Creditor Number 17's rent. Like the rent of all the families who moved here a few years ago before having children. We all live in apartments that have become too small and that we can hardly afford. We all know the next notification, next increase is coming.

I'm still looking into the sky. The crane sways to and fro, as if it had lost its mind. Take me with you, I call in the direction my penguin disappeared, but so softly that no one hears me, not even my dog, take me with you. Well, hurry up, it answers. Its voice sounds familiar. I push into the pedals and take up the chase.

I'm twenty years younger. It's winter, without snow, without sun, much too mild, much too gray. I lock my bicycle, an old Swiss Army bike, to a lamppost and enter the indoor swimming pool in my red pumps, the only shoes I own. The heat, the humidity, the smell of chlorine, all as expected; I loosen my scarf, unbutton my coat, take off my hat, and stare at the bare legs of the deeply tanned lifeguard, who's wearing only a shirt, shorts, and flip flops. He's taking his time with the customer at the register. She's speaking softly. He listens to her. He shakes his head. He makes swimming motions. They're talking about the crawl stroke, that much is clear. A dry-land swimming lesson. I'm hot. I turn around. Petrus, my first love, is standing behind me. He rolls his eyes heavenward and grimaces. And behind Petrus stands our mutual friend, I'll call him Simon. Murmuring, he strokes his neck. He wraps his hands around his neck and whispers in his deep voice: Right away, my sweet. He's not referring to me. Petrus knows this, but still asks: Did you just call my sweet your sweet? They punch each other in the upper arms. Every few days we go swimming together, Petrus, Simon, and I. Petrus leans toward me and gives me a kiss.

Now I'm back to Petrus. From penguin to Petrus. And now I recognize the voice. The penguin's voice in my ear. You never get free from your first love. It's nine months since I found out. I wrote Simon a letter, hand-written, and sent it to his Zurich address, which was still valid, according to the telephone book. I didn't get an answer. Did you know that Petrus jumped into the courtyard from the ninth floor as twilight fell one snowy evening? is the question I asked in my letter.

The kiss Philipp gave me this morning was sticky. I wiped it away, then wished I hadn't.

Can I have another?

That one didn't seem to your taste.

Yes it was. I just have to get used to it again.

Philipp went into the kitchen and put the children's oatmeal on the burner. I watched him. He knew I was watching but didn't turn toward me. He has the most beautiful back you can imagine. Well-shaped, straight, broad (but not too broad).

My dog is old. Ten years and eight months. She runs bravely along next to my bicycle. Her tongue hangs far out of her mouth, like in summer. I forget to cheer her on as has become my habit when she slows down next to me (as I do, too, until I almost fall off the bike), when she seems to have lost every last drop of joie de vivre and trots along dully, sluggishly. I forget because I want to catch up with the penguin, want to see him with his breast-band, and want to ask him what he's doing here, where he has come from and how he learned to fly. I've lost sight of him, but the direction is clear. I reach Alsterradweg behind the Dammtor station and there I catch sight of him, there he is, flying straight toward the main station, wait for me! and traffic on the Kennedy Bridge is thick, here! I shout and my dog follows my command to the letter, sticks close to my back wheel, together we throw ourselves into and across the street, reach the other side, have escaped once again, let's go, come on, run! and my dog briefly raises her head and smiles.

I dismount at the main station, wheel my bike across the station square and look in every direction, but the penguin is nowhere to be seen. Hurry up, I hear him say, your train leaves in five minutes! My hands tremble. It has never taken me so long to lock up my bike and put my dog on a leash. I run through hall and scan the display panel. I check my watch. In three minutes an Intercity Express leaves for Zurich on track fourteen. Zurich? Are you serious?

And then the penguin repeats the question, like Petrus always did: Am I serious? Dead serious!

The train departs. My dog stands on her hind legs and stretches her head to see out the window. Don't ask me where or why. I stroke her head and then realize that for the next eight hours there will be no opportunity for her to void herself. To relieve herself. To go out. To go "outsies" as they say in Austria, my dog is a native Austrian.

Can you wait that long?

She doesn't answer. She lies down. I close my eyes and breathe deeply. I smell chlorine.

In the mild gray winter a good twenty years ago, Simon, Petrus, and I were in a love triangle. Although we insisted, outwardly and inwardly, that we were a couple with a friend in common.

Despite the warm, drizzly weather, we were freezing all the time. During the day, when Petrus and I were home reading or studying, we would meet in the kitchen every hour, turn on the oven, which was much more effective than the ancient heater, open the door and hop around in the warm, damp air, telling each other about what we'd just been working on. Then we each returned to our own room and kept working until we felt cold again. There was hardly any snow in the lowlands that year. Over New Year's Eve, Petrus and I were in the mountains, in his friend-from-university's parents' house. There the snow soon reached head height, but Zurich stayed gray. Simon saw in the new year alone in his apartment, drawing. After New Year's Day, the heating failed and there was no hot water. Simon informed his landlord, a friendly man in his early nineties, who was so hard of hearing it took Simon five tries to make the landlord understand which of his houses he meant. Simon put on the three sweaters he owned, one on top of the other, and decided to shower at the public swimming pool for the time being. We offered him our bathroom, but he said he wouldn't be comfortable. He often slept in our bed, but the idea of showering at our place made him *uncomfortable*. Come on. We laughed. But Simon could not be talked out of showering at the pool. Still, he did agree to take us with him. Petrus swam three kilometers freestyle every few days anyway and I, an occasional and sedate breaststroker, hoped for an opportunity to finally improve my technique. I watched the suntanned lifeguard's dry-land swimming motions carefully. At some point, without interrupting his conversation with his student or even looking at us, he took our money, handed us three keys on wristbands, and pushed a red button. With a slight push, the turnstile spun. On the other side, paths diverged. Simon and Petrus turned left to the men's changing room. In my clattering pumps, I headed straight for the pictogram with a dress.

Every few nights, Simon slept at our place. The three of us lay in my big bed. At first Simon had slept in Petrus's narrow bed, then came to us one night, sat perched on the side of the bed, and waited in the dark until we woke up.

The bed over there is too soft, my back hurts.

Be quiet and lie down, Petrus replied, rolled to the middle of the bed and fell back asleep. I didn't say anything but watched Simon stretch out on our bed. He stared at the ceiling, I stared at him. Petrus lay between us, snoring softly.

A name flits through my mind: Roswitha! That was his *sweet's* name. She also slept in our bed. She was always present.

Simon was a loner, but never alone. On him, very discreetly, lived Roswitha: a spotted, gray, fancy rat with a pink snout, pink ears, and pink paws that he called *my sweet*. Wherever he went, she would go, too. He was her host, he said. That's why Roswitha was certainly not a pet, but an essential animal. Obviously, Roswitha came to the swimming pool with us, where, even though she was a good swimmer, she was always kept in a locker. The reason had little to do with Simon's consideration for his fellow swimmers, as we first thought. No, he was worried about Roswitha, worried about her *sensitivity to chlorine*. He didn't want to run *any risks*.

Simon—the word *rat* may well evoke unsuitable images—was not a punk or a bum. Nor was he a nut-job, or even an animal rights activist. He had taken the rat Roswitha in after an old school friend had died a few months earlier from a heroin overdose that may or may not have been intentional. Simon and Petrus often spoke of this Robert. The most talented of us all, Simon said and Petrus replied: Yes, without a doubt, but that never interested him in the slightest.

When Robert was still alive, Simon was Roswitha's godfather. He did it as a favor to his friend, even though he thought this was ridiculous. Three things, that's all, Robert had demanded: You have to celebrate her birthday with her once a year, get her a proper Christmas present, and if anything happens to me, you'll have her around your neck. In Roswitha's case, that was meant literally. Simon had given his word, he had no choice. She didn't seem to mind. In one furious leap, she threw herself at his chest, circled once, and made herself comfortable on the nape of his neck. For all time, it seemed.

I have to call Philipp. I have to tell Philipp I'm going to Zurich! Who's going to pick up the children. My mobile phone has no reception. Outside, the flat countryside flows into an endless, brownish gray, smeary stripe. On the ass. You can kiss mine, all of you. *I'll take care of it*—nothing there! I won't take care of anything, not of anything or anyone, whether you ask me for money, love, understanding, trust, or concern: Forget it! There's no more care to be had, so long. Zurich, here I come!

The conductor opens the compartment door and asks for my ticket. I don't have one.

Where are you headed?

Zurich.

Beautiful city.

I don't say anything.

No need to look at me like that, I've never been there, he says. He pulls out his electronic device. So then, one adult, one dog.

Couldn't you overlook the dog?

Our floors haven't been as black as your dog for a long time. So then. On international stretches you pay the children second-class rate for the dog. He calculates. It takes a while. That's two-hundred-sixty euros eighty-five. Please.

Two-sixty eighty-five? I only want to go to Zurich, that's all! One way!

Yes, that will be two-sixty eighty-five.

For a few minutes all I can think is: Why did I get on this train?

The penguin speaks up. That's enough. Lean back and relax. Close your eyes.

I open my eyes wide. Where are you?

Where am I? Here, he says, I'm right here. Shhhh.

The winter his heating failed, Simon had been commissioned by an insurance company to create an *amusing* bird mascot for their advertising. He was a doctoral student in physics, but earned money as a draftsman. The marketing department of the insurance company called him several times and demanded he submit his sketches.

There are no sketches, Simon admitted to us in his bass voice one evening as we were setting the table. It's a penguin, I don't know any more than that. No idea what it'll look like. He uncorked the wine with a grimace.

Why a penguin of all birds? I asked. Simon sniffed at the cork, glanced up briefly, slightly irritated, and answered in a sepulchral voice: They walk upright and can't fly. They are the humans among birds. Their vertical aspiration appeals to us. Simon reached into the neck of his sweater, cork in hand. He rummaged around at chest height for a while, then his hand reappeared—without the cork. My pleasure, my sweet, he murmured.

You should come up with a name for the penguin, I suggested, maybe then it will take shape. Petrus had nothing but mockery for my suggestions. Wonderful, the penguin follows his creator's call! But Simon was completely serious and his voice dropped another half an octave: I already have a name.

I can't wait to hear this, Petrus scoffed. An animal tautogram, perhaps? Like Roswitha the rat!—How about Pius the Penguin! Pee-pee!

Simon smiled. Not bad, but his name isn't Pius, it's Petrus.

Forget about it, Petrus said.

No, I won't. Don't you walk upright?

Yes.

Can you fly?

Yes.

Puzzled, we look at Petrus, then we reached for our wine glasses, laughed, and drank.

The fact that man cannot fly distressed Petrus as much as it fascinated him. The stubborn, burning desire on the one hand, the awareness of futility on the other. Petrus said: Human creativity can imagine but cannot transform. Only someone whose powers, whose skill, whose capacities far exceed the human can turn man into a creature that can fly, and we call that someone God. As long as man dreams of flight, there is a god. And Petrus's voice seemed to brighten when he added: Keep an eye out for him, don't expect him to die anytime soon. I even believe he is immortal! And Simon, who had been listening to him with a smile, rose on to his tiptoes, reached for Petrus's head with both hands, drew it down, and kissed him solemnly on the forehead. You are the best, he said.

That was all long ago. I wanted to visit Simon when I was in Zurich for work, but he wouldn't let me in.

Go away, he said through the intercom, leave.

Simon, what's wrong.

Just leave, he repeated, that's something you're good at.

I lean my forehead against the cold, streaky window and look outside. Winter will soon be here. What a rotten, dreary fall it has been! Colorful leaves only fell from the copper beech, and had already turned red in spring, but they'd been swept away long ago. What's ahead of me? There are days when I see possible creditors everywhere. In every phone call, every passerby, every fleeting glance, every neighbor, every friend. And now? I'd like to have my own apartment. My own mailbox. No one else's mail, no one else's problems, no one else's debts anymore. And my own new neighbors. My own apartment? Thinking about that is a waste of time. We share all our expenses, always have. With two households, they'd skyrocket. Philipp's salary is just enough to cover his half and a debt repayment plan. If I pulled out, he would never be able to climb down from his pile of debts.

My dog whines. What's the matter? She shuffles and dances and leans against the compartment door. Do you have to go? Don't joke around! We have five more hours on the train! She whimpers.

Stop, I say. That's enough, stop! I turn back to the window.

She lies down with a sigh. She curls into a ball and closes her eyes.

I sigh, too. Close my eyes and press a kiss onto the glass.

They don't seem to your taste.

Yes they are. I just have to get used to them again.

I dial Philipp's number. As I count the rings, I see the penguin fly by window. I'll be right back, it says.

Philipp surprises me again and again. When he hears I'm in a train to Zurich, he's happy. He'd like to travel now too, he says, and Zurich is always beautiful. He'll pick up the kids from nursery school, no problem. He's looking forward to a *boys' night* with his two sons. He asks if I wanted to visit my brother in Zurich.

Yes.

Then give him my best.

I will.

And get some rest.

I'll try.

And don't forget me.

I won't.

I wish I could open the window. Even in an emergency, it wouldn't be possible. This kind of high-speed train, with its sleek abbreviation of its ponderous name, is about as old as my memory, in fact, I believe I remember it first ran on exactly this route from Hamburg to Zurich in early 1992, that is, in the very same drizzly winter during which I shared my bed with Petrus and Simon.

It was a rainy February night. We lay close together, listening to the sound of the rain through the window we'd opened a crack, and looked into the future. That's what we called it. The three of us stared at the ceiling as if we could read the future on it. We would live together. We would wake up together, eat breakfast, go to the university. We would go swimming together at least every three days. Evenings, we would cook or go out. Go out dancing. To the movies, to art openings, to parties. We'd have friends. We'd constantly meet interesting people. At some point, Petrus, who was lying to my right, turned his head toward Simon, who was lying to my left, and said over me: If anything ever happens to me, take care of her, I'd like you to step in, right? "Her" was me. I lay between the two of them, still staring at the ceiling, but I felt Simon nod. I heard him clear his throat and then he said in his deep voice: Yes, I promise. He reached for his neck and put Roswitha gently in a cardboard box on the night table. He turned to me and gave me a kiss on the cheek. I turned to Petrus and passed the kiss on. Petrus leaned over me and kissed Simon first, then me. We all kissed each other, then touched each other, everywhere (while Roswitha waited in her box since I had made it a condition: no contact with the rat), then we all fell asleep. Yet we never spoke about it. Not to anyone. Certainly not to each other. It was our secret, which we kept even from ourselves.

Petrus and I were usually already asleep when Simon took his Roswitha out of her box and put her back around his neck, where she remained the rest of the night. Not once did she leave his neck without permission or come too close to me. All I ever got was a hint of her scent, a cozy whiff of hay with a slight, sharp, unsettling splash of urine. Roswitha remained monstrous to me. The only experience I'd had with rats before her had occurred a half-year earlier, and was still a blood-soaked memory: Petrus's brother bitten by a wounded rat in a French sheepfold after he shot an air gun recklessly in the dark of night.

Idiot, Simon had said when we told him the story one evening, what an idiot, unbelievable. I'm sorry for insulting your brother, he turned to Petrus and added, but I can't think of any other word to describe him.

That's all right, Petrus said, and smiled so tenderly that I became irritated.

Simon dropped his gaze and stroked Roswitha, my sister in fate, whom he inherited just as he would inherit me if anything happened to Petrus. As my eyes followed Simon's hand on Roswitha's fur, I imagined a possible future in which I was that rat. And the idea wasn't all that bad.

I must have fallen asleep. My dog woke me, she's thirsty. She laps up mineral water from the hollow of my hand—she briefly shrank back from the prickles but her thirst prevailed.

Outside the window, the Black Forest slides past. Autumn has no effect on it. Yes, I must have fallen asleep, soon we'll reach Freiburg. I close my eyes and let myself slip back into my dream. Dream? No, it wasn't a dream, it was a memory.

Over Petrus's protests, Simon called his mascot—when the bird finally took shape and did, in fact, resemble a penguin, with its elongated, lanky torso and stout abdomen in black tie and tails—Petrus.

Petrus couldn't believe it. Simon, I told you very clearly, that I don't want you to do that, he said.

Oh come on, Petrus, it's just a cartoon character.

You're jeopardizing our friendship for this laughable mascot!

Keep your shirt on, you're not the only Petrus in the world. And at some point Simon dropped that attractive phrase, *artistic freedom,* upon which Petrus asked him to leave our apartment. For two weeks, there was no Simon in our lives. Then one evening, he appeared on the doorstep and promised to give his penguin another name, though he didn't know which one at the moment and if absolutely necessary it would have no name at all.

I think Petrus was more insulted by the penguin's appearance than its name. The penguin not only had the same name, it looked like him. Too plump below, too lanky on top, with a stiff back and sloping shoulders, its head in the clouds.

Simon explained his drawing when he was allowed back in our lives. Of course, he didn't allude to the visual resemblances between Petrus and the penguin. No, he said: Penguins can live up to fifty years, even though their average life expectancy isn't very high, approximately twenty-five. That's all the more surprising since it has no natural enemies, only itself.

What do you mean by that, Petrus asked, do penguins all kill themselves midlife?

It seems that way, Simon said, and we tried to figure out how penguins would do that. Our mood was giddy, but Petrus didn't find any of the suggestions convincing. All that's left is for them to jump off a snowy peak, he concluded, but for ritual penguin suicide there are hardly enough suitable icebergs.

We went to bed, lay awake and silent, fell asleep at some point, dreamed, at least I did, of the view from the ten-meter diving board, and the next morning we went swimming. The smell of chlorine stuck to us that entire winter. It hung in our hair, on our skin, it was caught in our sheets, sat down at the table with us, wafted out of the refrigerator, out of the medicine cabinet in the bathroom, out of our bags, yes, even from our books.

When I think of our trips to the swimming pool, I can see the lifeguard before me almost more clearly than Petrus or Simon. It's astonishing how these minor, actually, completely marginal characters are preserved so clearly, so stubbornly, with such sharp contours and vivid colors! This lifeguard with his dark-brown calves covered with blond hairs and his blue-eyed monitoring stare that didn't miss a thing—unless he was cleaning, which was part of his job, even though he'd rather have hidden that. He would disappear without a sound and reappear just as silently after a time, scold a few children and return to his lookout on the pool edge. Once, while he was mopping the floor, he was puzzled by signs of life from a locker and went to get the master key. Roswitha the rat escaped. He caught her, apparently with a cleaning cloth, and threw her into the bucket, from which he had been kind enough to dump the dirty water first, as he put it. Then he called the police. He wanted to file a report, he told them, and talked about having to notify the health department. It was an outrage that someone would introduce a carrier of bacilli and filth like this rat into the public swimming pool. At the word *introduce,* we pinched each other in the arm and tried not to laugh. The rat darted this way and that in the red bucket. Its entire body trembled. We stood in a circle around her. It was my first time in the men's changing room. My pumps left tracks that couldn't possibly have come from a man's shoes. Big bulbous spots and under them little round circles. The lifeguard ignored them, as he did me. We waited for the police. The rat spun like a dervish in its plastic bucket. The police were not interested in the rat or in us. The lifeguard forbade us from entering the building ever again.

We hadn't even showered. We smelled of chlorine. We lay in bed and warmed up. Simon stroked Roswitha and described the future in his deep voice: When the rat is gone, I'm going to get myself a bird. Actually, Roswitha's not my type, I'm more of a bird-person, but a godchild is a godchild, what can I do? He gave her a kiss. My sweet. Your successor may well be a pigeon. He turned to Petrus: Assuming that I won't have to succeed you! Petrus didn't answer. He lay motionless. He loved to play dead and he was very good at it.

Twilight is falling. We'll reach Basel soon. It gets light a minute later every day now and dark a minute earlier, until there will be hardly any daytime left.

What are the children doing now? Philipp is picking them up from nursery school right now. Dressing them in their snowsuits with reflective stripes. Taking them to the supermarket to shop for the boys' night, chips and dip and popsicles.

Hello, I'm back! someone calls and a dark shadow flutters at the window. The penguin is back.

Where'd you go?

Where did I go? I had things to do.

Don't you want in?

In? Gladly, if you open the window.

Oh right, no, the window doesn't open.

Doesn't matter. I'm fine. The fresh air is doing me good.

Petrus?

Yes?

So he did name you Petrus!

Who?

Simon, your creator!

Have you got a problem with that?

Yes! No. What will we do in Zurich?

What will we do? We'll visit him.

Who?

Who? My creator.

It's just before seven when he opens his door. The train pulled into Zurich's main station at six o'clock on the dot. As I was getting out of the train, my dog yanked me onto the platform in one leap. I twisted my ankle. She tore to the nearest pillar on which, for the lack of a tree, she peed longer than she ever had before: I watched as the red hand of the station clock made a complete circle. The dark puddle spread strongly and rapidly over the platform. *Goddamn disgrace,* the passersby scolded.

Simon looks at me. Then at the dog. Again at me.

Hoi, I say. Hoi, the penguin echoes in my ear and it sounds stupid.

Simon looks at me.

I had eight hours to decide what to say, how to begin, but the only thing that occurs to me is *hoi*. He looks at me. He appears to be thinking. He has gotten old. His hair sparse, his lips thin, his cheeks hollow. Only his voice is unchanged. Dark, full, warm. Long time, he says.

I nod. I wrote you a letter.

He nods. He turns and walks away.

The door is open.

The dog is stretched out under the table. The penguin is in my ear. I stand there indecisively. Simon puts two cups on the table.

Sit down.

I keep standing.

He looks at me. Comes closer, stands right in front of me. He smells odd, but good. I know that smell, but I can't place it. He pulls me to his thick sweater, I claw my fingers into it, a sob rises. Simon's back shudders. I squeeze, he squeezes, it cuts off our breath. We breathe heavily, shaking, we weep because we can't help it, weep until we can't any more. What do you want to know? he asks.

Why he did it, I answer falteringly. He. Petrus's name still hasn't been said.

Simon looks at the cups. The tea has gone cold, he says. Doesn't matter, I answer and sit down.

Simon reaches for his cup. I don't know anything, he says between two sips. Only a little, he corrects himself. When did you last hear from him?

He wrote me at some point that he had stopped smoking, I say. Simon nods.

Why would someone quit smoking if he's going to jump out the window?

Simon nods.

Why are you nodding?

I'm nodding?

Yes.

Simon shakes his head. That was long before he jumped. I can still remember how Petrus called and said that he'd soon be forty, it was time to quit. And then there was a strange pause and I asked: Quit? Quit what? And Petrus laughed and said: Puff, puff, puff—smoking! Simon looks at me. Then he bends down under the table and asks my dog if she's all right. He kneels next to her and starts petting her. You're very soft, he says. I watch his hands stroke her dark fur. I remember the rat. Simon smiles. Roswitha? She's been dead almost twenty years. Don't look so horrified, fancy rats don't have a long lifespan.

And now? Do you keep birds?

Simon gives me a long look. No, he says. No, I live alone, still, as always. Sometimes I think I should find someone to live here with me but—no, I stand alone. Walk alone, lie alone. My dog has rolled onto her back and is relishing being petted, now and then she grunts softly.

And Petrus? How did he live, and with whom? I ask.

Simon shrugs. We were rarely in touch all those years after you split up. He withdrew. I didn't understand why, I still don't.

I close my eyes. Hear the shrill blast of the lifeguard's whistle. I watch Petrus, how he plows through the water with his long torso, it looks very easy. His arms swing up and down. As if he were flying. Simon sits on the edge of the pool. I can't anymore, he says to me. But take a look at Petrus!

A bird calls. That's the pied flycatcher, Simon says, that means it's nine. The wall clock behind him has pictures of birds instead of numbers. The big hand is vertical, the little hand is horizontal pointing left.

I excuse myself, go to the bathroom, and write Philipp a message: Arrived safely, good night. Then I call my brother. My brother doesn't pick up. I turn off my phone. When I come back into the kitchen, Simon takes a look at my sturdy boots and says: You have sensible shoes on! Is that because of age or wealth? Before you wore that pair of heels with straps all year long.

Because I still have no money, it must be because of my age, I reply. Simon looks at me: Are you spending the night?

Do you have room?

Yes.

We lay next to each other and stare at the ceiling, as if we could read the past on it. My sweet, Simon says in his bass voice and both of us listen: my dog next to the bed, me in it. He meant the dog. He strokes her. Then he asks: Where were you on November 17, 2008? What were you doing?

I was pregnant and suffering from nicotine withdrawal, I reply. And I thought of Petrus and how it was so easy for him to quit. Unlike me. The only sentence I could come up with was: Where can I get my next cigarette? The only sentence I could write was: I want to smoke. And that didn't stop for almost an entire year. Petrus, however, has simply quit. And I thought: Everything always came easy to you, you wealthy snob. You pseudo-bohemian. You amateur smoker.

Simon shakes his head. Did you really think that?

I shrug.

In our last conversation, Petrus told me his apartment was above the city tree line, Simon says. He said he lived at the same level as the birds and they circled in front of his window. He was perched there like an albatross in the doldrums. I've got no wind under my wings. Although in reality he was in fact a flying wonder! If he could just get airborne, he could ride out the wildest storm! I told him that albatrosses were not only very good flyers, but also fantastic swimmers, even in the heaviest swells. I know, Petrus answered me, I didn't choose the albatross arbitrarily.

Simon turns to face me. I no longer expected you to show up, he says, but I'm happy that you finally came. And now I recognize the smell. Strange, but good: Hay with a slight splash of urine. At the same time, cozy and unsettling.

10

Gray, a few degrees above zero

My son is on the line, the big little one.

Mama, are you there?

Yes.

Where are you?

In Zurich.

Where you lived when you were a child?

Exactly.

What are you doing there? Are you going to nursery school?

The connection is bad. I go outside. Gray, a few degrees above zero.

No, I'm working.

But your computer's here!

Yes, that's true, but you know, I'm writing by hand.

How?

Well, with a pencil!

With your hand?

No, with a (I stretch lips and over-enunciate) penn-ssill!

It's not cold, but I'm shivering. My jacket is inside the restaurant. I look in through the plate glass window. Only attractive people sit in the window. When the guests come in, they're divided up. The unattractive ones are led straight to the back. If an unattractive one is sitting near the window, he must be extremely rich or famous. Without the slightest hesitation, we were shown to a table in the very back of the restaurant. At the table next to us was a pudgy glutton who paid as quickly as he ate and then left.

I've been in Zurich for twenty-six days and nights. Simon offered his bed on the first night—it was, in theater jargon, a *reprise*. He never asked how long I was planning on staying. He went to the museum with me to see the Giacometti. To see the collection on Sunday, like before. But now it's no longer free. Fifteen francs. Simon paid for me. He walked inconspicuously at my side. As is his way. He says nothing, asks no questions, he doesn't seem to be interested or bored, he's simply there, at my side. I have looked for my favorite sculptures but not found them. *Striding Man. Dog. Falling Man.* All three are out in the world somewhere on loan. The falling man, my favorite from that time. I stood for several minutes in the spot where I believed it used to stand, in the middle of the room, stared into the emptiness, and remembered. The falling man is the size of a newborn, you could take him in one arm, but his proportions are different. A rail-thin, full-grown man as big as a baby, no orientation, swirling, at every moment about to fall into the void. The longer I stared at him the way I used to, unable to come to his aid, the more completely the room around me would dissolve, the more I myself had the feeling that there was no solid ground under my feet, that I was caught in a maelstrom and about to tumble with the spindly man.

My big little one (four-and-a-half) has handed the telephone to the little little one (two-and-a-quarter).

Mama? Are you?

I'm in (I stretch my lips again) Zuu-rich!

Here, give it to me, I hear my husband's voice. There's rumbling. Philipp's on.

Hello?

Yes?

Where are you?

In the art museum.

Alone?

With my old love, Alberto.

What?

A joke. Alberto Giacometti. Of course I'm alone, Philipp!

I had a dream about you, at first I didn't even recognize you.

Why not?

No idea. We've been together such a long time and I didn't recognize you.

Maybe it was too dark.

I dreamt you weren't coming back. You are coming back, aren't you?

Of course.

When.

I don't know yet. How's your mother?

She sleeps. She's weak. But when the radiation treatments are done, she'll be better—

Give her my best.

She'll get better, do you think so, too?

I take a deep breath. I hope so, Philipp.

I go inside. The waiter looks me over like he did earlier and gives me a confirming nod when I head toward my seat in the back.

Simon puts his cup down and waves at me. I smile at him. The table is taken again. The young woman who sits down is very pretty, what is she doing here? Someone that pretty belongs in the window! The old man with her is, at least from the side, truly hideous. Her beauty is no match. The old man turns his face toward me. Tadeusz! I drop my phone. I bend down, straighten up, and take another look: it's Tadeusz! He doesn't recognize me. Crazy. He looks at me—looks away—at me—away: He Doesn't Recognize Me!!!! The knocking sets in. Brutal Morse code tapping. Hammering in my head: - / * * / - - / * : TIME, as so often, and again: TIME. Then, after a pause: SMOKE. I stand there like the falling man, at least it feels that way. What's wrong? Simon asks and stands up, comes to me, takes my hand, blocking my view of Tadeusz. Nothing, I say, just the phone. I sit down.

Did something happen at home? To your children?

No, I dropped it.

Simon takes my phone from me and examines it. I peek at the next table. Unbelievable, the right name, the right man at the right time. Wonderful, Tadeusz is saying. Yes, that was his word, it was then and it still seems to be today: wonderful. The beautiful, the accomplished, the artistically inspiring: wonderful! With his Polish accent that he still has after forty years. Wonderful. What is he doing here? And who is the young woman? Why ask? I know all too well. She's his student. He's the famous director who also *vorks* on acting and directing as a professor. (It was never clear if Tadeusz was playing up his accent or not.) But why in Zurich? He was teaching in Berlin. Years ago, when I last heard from him. When he called me up and asked me to send him my play. He sounded impatient, greedy, as he always did when he wanted something; he had *stumbled*, he told me, on a review of the premiere in the newspaper. I'll send it to you, I said but I never did. He asked for it again two times and two times more, I promised to send it right away. Two more times after that, the secretary of the university wrote to remind me, then I was left in peace.

The student laughs. She has a high, clear, sparkling laugh. Tadeusz leans toward her and murmurs something to her. Conspirators. Tadeusz was born the same year as my father, a fact I found so unpleasant when I was his student that I haven't forgotten it. His students are always the same age, next to them he's geriatric. At the time, he was twice as old as I was, now he's three times as old as she is. Grandfather and granddaughter. Don't these artists ever retire, not even when they've become professors? Sitting there, over seventy and murmuring into a student's ear. Why is this beautiful young woman wasting the best time of her life, throwing away thousands of precious moments in her young life on this worn-out, washed-up old man? Apparently he's still worth it.

She's making time for him. Did he say: Hello, this is Tadeusz. Would you have a little time to spare this afternoon? Did she answer: I'll just make time, Tadeusz?

Simon has disassembled my mobile phone. He rubs each part, even the tiniest piece with a cloth handkerchief and blows the dust away from every angle. That should help, he says, and starts to put the device back together again. The hammering in my head hasn't changed.

Does Tadeusz not recognize me or has he not seen me? I think back to the train yesterday, when I retraced the route I took to school. It was Saturday morning, aside from me, only new recruits were up and about. They used to be a reason to wait for the next train. Today I can safely sit next to them, they look right through me. They can keep trading their misogynistic banter at the top of their voices, why not? I'm invisible.

For Tadeusz, too, it seems. Only Simon can see me, his smile is a clear sign, apparently I still exist.

Tadeusz and I last saw each other more than seven years ago when I'd just met Philipp, at about the same time we decided to get married, almost exactly two days after Philipp and I called the registry office and applied for a marriage license. He ran into me by chance at the Bahnhof Zoo station, just before slipping into insignificance (the station, that is), the morning after I'd done a reading from my first book. In those days, I was so deeply in love that I gave just about everyone I met an enthusiastic hug. Even Tadeusz, when he unexpectedly appeared right in front of me. We hadn't seen each other for a few years. He didn't hesitate long, seized the offer and grabbed me, kissing me on the mouth. I pressed my lips together. After I'd wrenched myself free from his embrace, he said, Forgive me, with a grin I can only imagine he thought was irresistible. Forgive me, grin. Then he immediately tried again, another frontal attack on the target, tongue out.

Stop it, Tadeusz!

Now you sound the same as before, too bad, he retorted curtly.

The telephone won't turn back on. There's no response, no matter which button you push, no matter how hard or how long you press it. Simon, patient, plucks it apart again, examines the parts, cleans them, almost mechanically, with his blue checked handkerchief, concentrating intently. I'll figure it out, he murmurs.

Tadeusz waves at the waiter. Another round? The beautiful student nods. Tadeusz puts his hand on her. His hand lies there—I count to five—then she gently pulls hers out from under it.

Later he claimed that he had seen me at Bahnhof Zoo, run after me, but missed me when I boarded the Intercity-Express to Munich, *the doors will close automatically, please exercise caution before departure.*

I told my friend Nathanael about it. Your professor is dreaming, he said, or else he's hallucinating: Long distance trains haven't stopped at Bahnhof Zoo for quite a while! That was five years ago.

Now he sits there and doesn't recognize me. Have I changed that much? I've gained weight since I quit smoking. I tried to avoid this humiliation, I tried to fast while I was dealing with the withdrawal, but I was pregnant and hungry, and I failed. I gained weight constantly, inexorably. So much that I'm unrecognizable? Despite similar clothing, the same hair cut? Not likely. It's more a question of age than weight. I'm seven years older. I'm not a young woman anymore. Keeping the same haircut makes no difference: I'm neither seen nor recognized.

I look at the way Tadeusz looks at this beautiful young student. Music, they're playing music here, which I didn't even notice before. The song that's playing right now, I know it, it's a lovely song. It came out when I met Philipp. Yours is the first face that I saw, Conor Oberst sings in a wavering voice, I think I was blind before I met you. Tadeusz doesn't seem to hear it. He's talking to the beautiful student insistently, looking at her insistently all the while.

His observations fascinated me. When I was this student's age and he was my professor, when I sat with him for hours after rehearsal for *debriefings* in which he never spoke about the production, but insisted on telling me about amazing coincidences, situations he had witnessed, amazing things that happened to him. Wonderful, he'd cry, simply wonderful: I was crossing the courtyard to the stage door, lost in thought about the rehearsal, which was about to start—and for which I was drawing a complete blank—and at that very moment an entire set of shelves was being pushed across the courtyard, you know, on one of those wheeled dollies, a so-called *dog*, with several shelves full of life-sized heads we'd had made for the production but then rejected. All of us, the whole team, had modeled for them. Now they're clattering and rattling past me: my actors, my assistants, all bodiless, nothing but heads. The shelves were piled one after the other on the back seat and passenger front seat of a parked car. When I pass it, I see myself on the passenger seat, cheek to cheek with the dramaturge. I stare at myself wide-eyed and my head seems to be nodding at me. I nod back and look around quickly to see if anyone is watching, and there's the make-up artist. She grins at me and says: Tadeusz is greeting his own blockhead. I reply: What are you planning on doing with the heads? We're sending them to one of the rehearsal stages for another production, she says. No way, I say, the heads belong to us. I reach in and grab mine, then go to the rehearsal. I suddenly knew what to do. My wooden head saved the production!

I'm glad I didn't die before I met you, Conor Oberst sings but no one is listening to him. I think of Philipp. This song back then. When we didn't really know each other but were setting out into the future together. When I was still so light he could easily lift me in the air. When he moved as supply as a cat, surefooted even at dizzying heights. Now I don't know where I am / I don't know where I've been / But I know where I want to go, Conor Oberst sings.

And now? I ran off twenty-six days ago, when Philipp kissed me. When he gave me the kiss I'd waited more than half of a year for. I'm visiting my brother, I said to him and repeat it daily on the phone to him and my two small sons. Though I'm staying with Simon. I'm banking on the fact that Philipp won't call my brother and ask. Philipp doesn't really want to know things. Especially not when they might make him unhappy. I've suffered because of it for seven years and now I'm taking advantage of it.

Philipp doesn't reproach me at all. You need space, he explains so that I don't have to explain anything to him. You need space for yourself and peace and quiet to write. That's true. He told his mother I'm doing research for my next book. That's true, too. His mother lives with us now. She can get radiation therapy just as well in Hamburg, no problem, she says. She cooks for the boys at night, sings songs, plays with them, reads to them, puts them to bed. She probably lets them watch television, doesn't make them clean their rooms, doesn't brush their teeth properly and gives them milk with honey afterward, no problem!

She can't make it through the day without taking at least one nap. If she goes shopping, it takes her at least an hour and she comes home pale and exhausted. When she cooks, she has to sit down every few minutes.

How are you doing?

I'm doing great, I really am!

And the therapy isn't too tiring?

No, it's really not, no problem at all!

Philipp ignores her condition. Mama, wouldn't you like to cook us some delicious potato soup? Philipp can't bear to see her weak. Here, the socks, could you please darn them? Philipp is afraid. Mama, I put the shopping list for tomorrow on the table. He runs his hand through his thick, dark hair. She'll get better, don't you think?

We just have to wait and see, Conor Oberst sings, and I nod. Everything OK? Simon smiles at me. Stubborn case, he says and points at my mobile phone. Seems to have fallen into a coma. Maybe it's nothing that dramatic, I say, maybe it's just hibernating. Then I'll tickle it awake, Simon says and pulls out his pocketknife, snaps it open and starts working on the telephone with the blade.

We just have to wait and see, I say, and I think of a black cat.

Tadeusz laughs. He sounds hoarse. Now you've got it, he calls out happily. The student agrees. I think I see a shadow of contempt for this self-satisfied old man flit across her smile. Or did I conjure it there and only I can see it? There are things one doesn't see immediately, Tadeusz says at the next table, tapping his forehead with a finger—things one only gradually recognizes, that's what work is!

His wife told me she found out every time when she called me one day. First, she asked if I was the one on the phone, before she gave her name then added: the wife of the man you're having an affair with. You forgot your mascara in his room. Do us both a favor, please, and don't bother denying it. Don't be as small-minded as the phalanx of your predecessors. Above all, don't be so naïve as to think Tadeusz is able to love anyone. The only problem is that I love him, have for twenty-four years, despite everything, I still do, I've never stopped loving him. When he got here, he was nothing. I'm the one who taught him German, who introduced him to the theater circles, found him his first assistant, got him out of bed in the morning and drove him to rehearsals, chose plays for him, suggested concepts and casts, held his hand during the premieres, and brought him home after the parties completely out of his mind. I supported him, nagged him, pushed him, because Tadeusz is not a person who has any idea what the next step is. I always put him on the right path and I'm not going to let him go astray. What can you give him? Nothing. And you can't expect anything from him either: there is no Tadeusz without me and I will destroy you. Get your hands off my husband. Keep your distance. And finally: I hope that someday, somewhere deep inside, you feel what it's like to have another woman steal your husband.

I'm not planning on getting married, sorry, but thanks for the good wishes, I said. No, that's what I would have liked to say. As far as I can remember, I said nothing at all.

She was about to hang up and added: You really roughed him up. All those bruises, you think that's fun? What kind of a person are you?

I was shocked, speechless, and completely confused. I wanted to call Tadeusz but hesitated, fretted over it for hours and finally let it go. He called me the following day. He sounded light-hearted and wanted to see me.

Tadeusz had occasionally talked about his wife. He never referred to her as *my wife* but always as *Ute* even though I'd never met her. Ute was an incredibly talented journalist. Along with her demanding job, Ute took care of her elderly parents, with whom she lived on an enormous farm with countless pets and farmyard animals, but no livestock since Ute was, aside from everything else, an engaged animal rights activist. But: Ute was wrong. I had no relationship with Tadeusz. I don't know why I didn't set her straight. Was it because of her opening? Tadeusz knows I'm calling you, she'd told me at the start, he gave me your number himself and agreed that I call.

Or was it just that I didn't want to interrupt her, in order to find out as much as possible?

Tadeusz was having sex with a violent woman. It wasn't me. But who could it be? And when did he have time anyway? When we were in rehearsals I wasn't the only one watching him, the whole team was. He spent his free time with me and, on weekends, he went home! What was with the mascara? Whose was it? And the bruises? I wanted to find out. I watched Tadeusz closely, I leafed through his notebook, pricked up my ears when he was on the phone, suspected every woman in the room with us, but got no results. I tried to imagine: I bit the nipples of a man my father's age, who had a body similar to his but with Tadeusz's head, until they bled. I pinched him with pliers until he writhed. I beat his testicles with a blunt object until he begged for mercy. I pressed a lit cigarette into his navel until he screamed. I didn't enjoy it and wasn't really convinced, so I gave up. I kept meeting Tadeusz. We never spoke of his wife's phone call. But her call changed everything. He started giving me money for taxis. Way too much. What is he paying me for? I asked myself. One evening, Tadeusz started stroking my head. Sometimes I have the feeling we've known each other forever, he said. He kissed me on the forehead. You're beautiful. His lips wandered down to my cheeks, kissed them, moved on to my lips, kissed them, too, gently, very gently.

From that evening on, he tore my clothes off whenever we were alone, demanded that I undress him just as roughly, that I sit on him and—he had very clear ideas—abuse him according to his directions. I left early in the morning when he was asleep. The taxi drivers raced through the night. Tadeusz could only drive at a walking pace at night on the small access road that led to Ute's enormous old farmhouse. He told me that she made him do this so that he wouldn't run over any animals.

One night Tadeusz started working away at my rear end with a smooth, cool object. When the pain became unbearable, everything was warm and damp and covered with blood. After that I avoided him. Tadeusz begged me to forgive him, howled night after night into the phone and into my ear, he charged himself with being a goddamn criminal, a lunatic, a repulsive pig. I stayed away.

Simon can't do it. The cell phone gives no sign of life. He says he'll have to look around at home to see if he has any manual for this kind of device. It's time to get back for my sweet anyway. He means my dog, whom we left in his apartment because we couldn't bring her into the museum with us. The poor thing has been alone long enough. Are you coming or are you going to stay here?

Simon loves my dog. It's not easy for her at home. Philipp takes his frustration out on her, the boys are rough, they pull her ears when I'm not looking or push her away when she trots up to them to be petted. She's not allowed on playgrounds, the boys don't want to go on long walks, and because there are two of them and they scream louder, they usually win.

But Simon speaks to her softly with his dark cellar voice. He praises her. He pets her. He takes her for walks, plays with her. He has bought her food and a brush, dog chews and a blanket because we arrived at his place without any baggage. An old dog is expensive. He was able to order the eye drops she needs twice a day for her autoimmune disease that will eventually make her blind from the specialist in Hamburg, even though his assistants were not thrilled about having to make an extra trip to the post office to send a package, complete with customs declaration, to Switzerland. And the day before yesterday he took her to the vet for her monthly manual cleaning of her anal glands, which are chronically blocked and inflamed, a procedure that stinks horribly. But Simon's love is great, so great that yesterday he tried to take away from her a chocolate wrapper that she'd found in a bush and greedily licked clean. I would never dare try because I know: Love stops when there's food. She bared her teeth, growled, snapped at him. A logical sequence. Simon couldn't believe it. He was shocked. The wound on the ball of his hand is deep. It's shocking to learn where the limits of love lie, to recognize its borders. A few minutes later, she lay her head in his lap as meek as a lamb.

I'm just going to stay a few minutes, Simon. I want to make a few notes.

About what?

About the exhibition and so on, I say.

I'll take sweet for a walk, he says, you've got a key.

I nod.

Can you manage without—he paused briefly—your phone.

I nod.

And without your sweet?

I nod.

And without—me?

I don't nod.

He puts a bill on the table.

See you later, Simon, and thanks. I watch him leave, pull my notebook out of my bag, open it on the table and pretend to write.

I concentrate on the conversation at the next table, but Tadeusz is speaking quickly and so softly that I can hardly understand a word. The beautiful student can't get a word in but seems to be interested in what he's saying. Again, Tadeusz puts his hand on hers. At what point are they in their relationship? How close have they become? Has Ute called her yet? I assume that over the course of their now more than forty years of marriage Ute has called each of the other women just like she called me. Maybe this is her refined way of leading playmates to her husband, women he can torture and be tortured by, and of very elegantly diverting the violence out of their relationship! Could that be the secret to their strong marriage? What do I know? I don't even know if they're still married.

Peering over at him works best with eyes almost shut. Tadeusz. He looks terrible. Wrinkled, gray, puffy, his entire face is slack and drooping. I don't know, is he sleeping? Does he eat anything besides sausage? Does he even wash himself? His greasy brown coat would suit a bum. Completely ratty, near the end. But honestly: Didn't Tadeusz look exactly like this twenty years ago, just twenty years younger?

Without being aware of it, my fake writing has turned into actual notes. Tadeusz came into a world at war, my notes say. Born in 1943 in occupied Warsaw. His father was imprisoned for being a Communist, sent to Auschwitz (he was lucky: The gassing of non-Jews—except for gypsies—was suspended) from there to another concentration camp every few months and on May 1, 1945, he was freed from a satellite camp of Dachau. His last station before returning to Poland was a displaced persons camp in Munich.

Tadeusz was three when his father came home, five when his father joined the Communist party, seven and just starting school when his father's doubts—seeing the Stalinist system—got the upper hand over his belief in Communism's capacity for reform. One day after the birth of his second child, his daughter Agata, Tadeusz's father gassed himself in their kitchen. Tadeusz was eight.

I peer at him from under my almost closed eyelids. I know all that about you and you don't even recognize me. I could even publish this, I could send what you confided in me out into the world, I could sell your story as mine.

My fascination with his life was strange for him, but I was stubborn, and because men like it when others are interested in them, I found out what I wanted to know. In fact, I learned more than I wanted to. At eight, Tadeusz took care of baby Agata and his mother, whose son he no longer was. He was her companion, her protector, her comforter. Early in 1968, he joined the student protest against the cancellation in the national theater of an anti-Soviet play by Adam Mickiewicz. *Independence without censorship!* the students demanded, and that sparked the March events in Warsaw. Disillusioned by the rigidity of the political system, though far less despairing than his father, Tadeusz applied for an exit visa that October. His goal was West Germany, more exactly, Munich, the site of his father's captivity and liberation. After a few days—Tadeusz claimed it was exactly seven—he met Ute at the university. She took him under her wing and, because he needed money and prospects, introduced him to some theater people. Tadeusz hadn't been especially interested in the theater until then. Taking part in the protests against the national theater in Warsaw had been a political, not an artistic or explicitly theatrical statement. So within a week, Tadeusz had found himself a wife, a job, and professional prospects. What a transformation story: a Polish student without goals, support, or means had turned into an aspiring theater director and husband.

As soon as I write about anyone's financial situation, I have to think of my own. For months I've done everything I could, taken every possible job to earn money: tutoring struggling seventeen-year-old students, writing articles for weekly papers and magazines—for *Gender Pages*, of all things, covering male-female issues, as if I knew something about this area or were an expert. At one point, two of my articles were going to appear on the same page, so the editor asked me to come up with a pseudonym. She was not kidding—I asked five times. I said: Fine, I'm Phyllis Plank. But first I have to check with my husband, since that's his name. Well, almost.

Philipp agreed right away. I wrote a piece in which I claimed I constantly had dreams about sex, despite an ancient, unverified and therefore untenable study making the rounds again that categorically denies women have such fantasies. And what happened? Philipp started having sex dreams. One morning, he said: Last night I had an erotic dream for the first time in ages. . . . We looked at each other, were immediately seven years younger and, if the little little one hadn't come into the kitchen right then with a full diaper . . . who knows!

After churning out only this kind of thing for a while, I need time to write, time for this book.

The student at the next table is on the phone. She chews her lower lip and says mmh, mmh, mmh. Her gaze is turned inward. Tadeusz orders himself a beer. What are the two of them doing here? Did they go to a Sunday matinee at the theater? Or maybe they went to the art museum, like we did? To the Giacometti? They came into the restaurant no more than five minutes after us. We'd have seen each other in the exhibition . . . The student says into her phone: OK, K, K, examining the fingernails on her left hand. Tadeusz drinks. Even the foam turns gray as soon as it touches his upper lip. Pale and leaden, it hangs between his nose and mouth, fits his face perfectly. I look around the room, over to the distant window where the beautiful sit and behind which lurks the gray winter day. The beer moustache would suit this colorless day just as well as it does Tadeusz. *But perhaps I am the prey, on the subject of grey, in the grey, to delusions.* . . . I read the sentence in a book I found on Simon's bookshelf yesterday: *Dialogue in the Void: Beckett & Giacometti.* A sentence from Beckett's *The Unnamable.*

Twenty years ago, I was given this book as a Christmas present, in that mild winter that was as gray as the day is today. I was delighted with it. I carried it around with me for a while in the inner pocket of my winter coat, the one that's meant for your wallet and lies next to your heart. And when I wanted to read it, it was gone. I found the book on Simon's shelves and asked: Your book?

Simon shrugged. Apparently. It got stranded here at some point or other.

There's a dedication in it: *For you from me.* I recognize the handwriting. It's my book!

Tadeusz suddenly stands up. So suddenly that the smell of cold frying fat wafts over to me. As if he'd spent the night in a McDonald's. Tadeusz rises onto the tips of his toes, lifts his arms out to the side and tries not to lose his balance. As he does so, he watches the student, who nods eagerly. It seems to be some kind of object lesson. Tadeusz sways, starts to tumble, rows with his arms. He looks like, unbelievable how much he looks like Giacometti's *Falling Man.* The one I'd looked for in the exhibition in vain, out in the world somewhere on loan.

I'm no longer looking at him out of the corner of my eye. I turn to face him and stare at him openly. At that moment, his expression changes. His age. His sex. His appearance. He is a young go-getter, a desperately suicidal woman, a dancer on the volcano, an ignorant and stubborn young lady. For a second he looks like my ailing mother-in-law. I can hear Philipp's voice: Don't look down! If you look down, you're lost.

Before Tadeusz falls forward, he stops. He looks at me. Tadeusz, I say. His face crumples. He blurts out: Wonderful, that's just wonderful!

Wonders are many, I think, as I had thought earlier when I heard him say, in his heavy Polish accent with its open vowels: But nothing is more wonderful than man.

Sophocles (Sahphocles!). Tadeusz laughs. He straightens up, spreads his arms and gives me a hug. I look over his shoulder at the beautiful student who is sitting there, smiling indifferently. Tadeusz hugs me tight and holds me close. Man, oh man, he cries, how are you?

11

Last trip

I dreamt about him last night. He said his name was Jakob. Jakob? My twelve-year-Jakob? No, he looked completely different, younger, more beautiful. Even more beautiful, since my twelve-year-Jakob was quite beautiful. But this Jakob last night. . . . There are men who are so beautiful your heart skips a beat when you see them—he was one of them. With fathomless green eyes, thick dark curls, prominent cheekbones and curved nostrils, soft lips and a slight gap between his front teeth. One of those. He seemed to know me. Does the time still work for you? he asked and I nodded. Good, then I'll pick you up at seven, as agreed, right? I nodded again or rather kept nodding. I was surprised not to have any idea about what we'd agreed on, but didn't want to ask in case he'd mistaken me for someone else. His accent was familiar. He came from Zurich, like me. But why was he speaking High German to me? So it was a mix-up? Looking forward to tonight, I said in dialect, but he just smiled awkwardly, the way Swiss do when foreigners try to speak in our idiom. Hello, I'm born and bred! Of course, he said in High German, see you at seven! And he disappeared. Who can hold a grudge against such beauty? Not me. I was out of my mind with joy, I trembled with happiness and excitement, stumbled into the bathroom and looked at myself in the mirror. The deep furrow in my brow. There was knocking. Hello? Who's there? Knocking.

Short / short short / long long / short

Short / short short / long long / short
Short / short short / long long / short

I grabbed my temples. Find something else to do instead of knocking, I said and switched off the light in the windowless bathroom. Darkness. Then this boy, this Jakob, I'll call him One-More-Jakob. No: Jakob Two. No: Jakob Junior. Yes: better than: Jakob Reloaded. Then this Jakob Junior opened the door and put his hand on my heart. Get your paws off, I said, but he didn't listen, quite the contrary. His hands were all over. But he suddenly stepped back. Excuse me, he said, I have to do something real quick. He pulled out his communication and data device and started jabbing hectically at the little screen, in the light of which his face glowed green but his eyes looked black and dead.

Jakob?

Not now, he hissed. I shrank back and straightened my sweater.

Later, we went to get something to eat. A candle flickered between us. His mouth shone, the wings of his nose quivered, trembled, wanted to take flight. Jakob Junior (should I go with a nickname? How about J.J.?) slid the tip of his tongue over the gap in his teeth as if to push out an intruder and pushed the candle aside. His mouth moved toward mine. Just before our lips touched, he shrank back and said (this time sounding not at all Swiss, but more like he was imitating the French waiter) that he forgot something. He jumped up, pulled his portable office from his pocket and hurried outside. Now I knew for sure. I recognized that behavior and had sworn to myself that I'd recognize it in the future, too. Now I was recognizing it even in my dreams.

Listen Jakob, I said when he came back to the table, were you, is it possible that you're playing?

He looked at me with his unbelievably green eyes.

You mean with you? he asked.

No, I mean, are you a gambler?

For several seconds a whole range of expressions flitted across his face, astonishment gave way to amusement, then outrage and fear. He laughed, denied, admitted.

I am, he said and his face relaxed. How did you know?

I'm married to a gambler.

Aha!

He had told me for years that his sudden bursts of digital activity were professional, that his job was demanding. He would suddenly remember something he had to take care of right in the middle of the nicest moments. And like in the theater: always a fire to put out. Nothing could ever wait. It was always something that had to be done immediately.

So your husband works in the theater? J.J. asked (it remains to be seen if the nickname will win me over).

Yes, I answered, on the set.

And what does he play?

Sometimes poker, usually he bets on sports.

Strange, J.J. (well . . .) says, just like me!

He joined in a conversation in which, because he was so eager to learn, I explained everything about my husband's gambling, at least as much as I knew, and about his debts, his therapy, and that's where my dream ended and I woke up.

My first thought was: The man of my dreams is a gambler—you get what you wish for, so to speak. I fell back onto my pillow, flipped onto my stomach, and buried my head in the pillows. Oddly enough, even though I was completely awake I was able, in this position, to continue my dialogue with J.J. (yes, I'm gradually getting used to it). I asked him how high his debts were (*manageable*) and whether he could cover dinner, since I had no money (*of course*). He didn't seem offended when I added: I don't need more than one gambler in my life. He waved the French waiter to our table, handed him his credit card, no longer speaking with a French accent, but pure stage German. He seemed to be a linguistic chameleon. However, the French waiter promptly handed it back. I'm sorry, Monsieur, we only take silver, gold, or cash, he said.

And so I paid, after all. It would have been too good: too beautiful a man, too beautiful an invitation.

My dog trots up to the bed. She stretches, perks up her ears, gives me a demanding look. I stand up. She jumps. If I, as an old lady, still look forward to mealtimes this much, then I'll be happy. My dog licks her chops. She drools. She leads me, prancing, to the kitchen.

I'm sitting in tram number 13, heading out of town. I'm going to visit my grandmother. She's on the Hönggerberg and it's the first time since she was buried that I've gone to see her. On Meierhofplatz I have to change to the bus. I wait for bus number 38 for more than half an hour, even though it goes on the half-hour and we are in—hello, where are we now?—Switzerland. In Hamburg, I wait for the bus for hours, but I won't put up with that here. It's Sunday, after all, there's no traffic, no snow—no ice, that is—no disruptions, no problems. I'm thinking about calling the dispatcher of the municipal public transportation that's listed next to the bus schedule, when I see the bus turn the corner. I am the only passenger, not counting my dog. The driver wishes me a lovely and peaceful third advent. I'm speechless. Then I say: You, too.

I've been in the city for more than a month without visiting her. Without having thought much about her. Even though I would claim that not a day goes by when I don't think of my grandmother, I know I didn't think of her once over the past few weeks. And I didn't miss her. Today, again, I feel like I'm just dropping in to see her in her kitchen on a Sunday afternoon on my way somewhere else, like I used to, without a present—she never had time for presents, stupid things, take it with you please—and naturally without flowers since she reacted to flowers as if she were highly allergic. Get them out of my sight! How much did you spend on them? You might as well have thrown your money away!

I can hear her voice in my ear and I have to laugh. You could not bribe my grandmother. She loved me, her other grandchildren weren't as lucky.

Love is not something you choose, dear heart. That's the sentence that echoes in my mind most clearly, the sentence she said more often than just about any other. Love is not something you choose. It was doubly true in her case. She liked Grandfather, she couldn't do anything about it. All he had to do was look at her and she said yes before he even asked anything. Yes. Yes to everything. And he was the only one interested. She was already over twenty, her parents were pressuring her, if you're an old maid, no one will want you. And so she married because she wanted to without really wanting to—and because she had to. This entire time, I'm thinking only of her, even though her husband lies next to her. When I visit her, I visit him. Grandfather. You are so pale, so very distant, you no longer have a face or a voice and yet you've only been dead a little longer than she has. Keep sleeping!

How did Grandmother do it? How did she love this man so deeply? He made life difficult at the end with his unbearable disgust with the world, his horror of everything human (himself included) and everything temporal. He would announce that he loved only God, the eternal, the perfect, the one God. It sounded especially poisonous when he said this in my grandmother's presence, with a sidelong glance at her and in a tone that was more final than death. His offensive behavior and pronouncements could not harm her love. Still, she wished for his death more ardently than she'd desired her wedding more than fifty years earlier. She could hardly wait for him to die and yet, when the time came, she didn't know what to do with her love and soon leapt after him.

Dogs aren't allowed in the cemetery. I tie my dog's leash to the fence and say: Wait. Be good. Don't bark. I take a few steps, turn and put my finger to my lips. My dog barks. Quiet, I call and hurry away. Just don't look back.

Grandmother and Grandfather are my only relatives who were buried. All the others were cremated and scattered or put on a shelf. My grandparents' plot will last for another year or two, then the "use period" will expire, eternity will be over, the lease will have run out, the house vacated (well, recycled, the bones will stay in the ground, they will be "properly buried deeper in the same plot") and rented out again.

I can't find it. I thought it would be impossible to forget the spot and the path leading to it, but now I'm wandering around the graveyard, with a map in my hands, on which the layout of the graves is indicated using letters for sections and numbers for the plots. I don't know the number of the plot or which section they're buried in. On Sundays the cemetery office is closed. Whom can I ask?

As long as Grandfather was still alive, Grandmother liked to talk about death, always about her own. How she wanted to be buried at sea. She had a lifelong yearning to be near water, a lifelong feeling that the mountains were beautiful but also alien, a lifelong apprehension that perhaps she might have come from somewhere else originally.

What a cabbage head, Grandfather would exclaim, where else could you possibly have come from? You're from Galgenen in Schwyz, period, the end.

What does he know, Grandmother would say so softly that he couldn't hear her, even as a little child I dreamt of the sea, *lighthearted, laughing child that I was.*

That's right, Undine, Grandfather would call out and Grandmother would answer: Why are you pricking up your ears? Read your newspaper.

But after Grandfather died, she never mentioned the sea again. It was clear that she would never leave him alone in his grave. Love for him had given her a soul, she said. *Loving and suffering and ensouled.* Once, when she asked me what I wanted to study after graduation, I answered *literature,* and she said: *There must be something beautiful, but also extremely awful about a soul. Would it not be better never to partake of one?*

What is that?

I would like to have that put on my gravestone.

But Grandma, you want to be thrown into the sea, where can they put a gravestone?

You're right, she said. But you should read *Undine* sometime!

I nodded and smiled and thought, what am I supposed to do with a tearjerker like that?

I've found it. I'm standing right in front of it. In my memory, it was completely different. Splendid and covered with flowers. Just two names and four dates and a practical evergreen. And now I'm completely shaken, and I have to concentrate with all my might on the two As in their first names not to break down and weep.

On the way home in the number 38 bus, I talk to Jakob Junior. Without my noticing, he had slipped into the seat across from me and gives me a slightly gap-toothed smile. Hello.

Oh, hello, what are you doing here?

Those eyes should be outlawed. That green, that look should at least be put under house arrest. Jakob Junior smiles and doesn't answer. (Actually we'd moved beyond that, onto nicknames. So:) J.J. smiles. J.J. doesn't answer (the nickname works!).

The bus driver is a different one, but he says the same thing: I wish you a lovely and peaceful third advent. His accent is from Sankt Gallen.

Isn't that strange, J.J.?

They've been instructed, he answers calmly, in the same Sankt Gallen accent as the driver. You'll never hear a spontaneous sentence from them. The reason is: They're preparing us for the robots that will be driving our public buses starting next year. Why are you calling me J.J.?

Robots? Are you serious?

He just looks at me. Opaque sunglasses, that's what he should be ordered to wear!

Why J.J.? he asks.

Because I already have one Jakob in my life.

What happened to him?

I left him to marry my husband.

The gambler?

Exactly.

That sounds like a bad trade, he says, a Jakob for a gambler. (That Sankt Gallen accent gives me the jitters!)

You should talk, you're both! Are you more Jakob or gambler?

Phew, that's too complicated for me, J.J. says and grins (this is new, he grins! And when he does, his soft lips turn into lovely, hilly landscape). I'd rather hear about your ex-Jakob!

He's an actor, I answer, and that is, in fact, the first thing that occurs to me. We met twenty years ago at the Theater Academy. Each person creates and shapes his or her own reality—we learned that there. But somehow our reality created a life of its own and wouldn't let us shape it. It did whatever it wanted to! And that was never actually what we wanted. (I tried out a grin, too.) For twelve years we were a couple, but lived in different cities for most of it, trying to have careers and to become rich and famous.

J.J. looks at me closely. I have the feeling you're treating me like a child, he says.

Like a child—I immediately start to feel maternal and that's the last thing I need. I'm not treating anyone like a child, I say, not even my two young children who have been waiting for me at home for a month, and before I start playing anyone else's mother I'm first going to catch up on what I've missed, got it? And since when do you come from Sankt Gallen?

He whistles appreciatively. Of course, he says. He ignores my last question. But back to your career, it didn't work out? he asks.

Well, you know, our standards were too high. Especially Jakob's.

I just wanted the opportunity to work with good people. He, however, wanted more: recognition, respect, influence.

And?

At some point there was too little that connected us but also too much for us to leave each other.

And?

I tried several times. One attempt was getting myself a dog.

This old mutt? He points to my dog who has curled up on the floor of the bus.

She's a regular beauty, isn't she?

That's clear. And then?

Another attempt was to fall in love. But that didn't work. Despite countless affairs. Until Philipp, my husband.

J.J. sighed. Love. . . , he began, but didn't finish the sentence.

What about love?

J.J. sighed. Sighing suits him spectacularly, too.

What do you know about love? You're much too young and much too beautiful.

Seriously, you think I'm beautiful?

Yes. You're the most beautiful man I've ever seen.

Then the congratulations go to you, you're the one who made me so beautiful.

No, you just appeared to me that way, complete and gorgeous, last night in my dream. The only thing I've done is transpose you into daytime.

And what will happen with us now?

We have to get off at this stop, come!

The number 13 tram is ready to go. We run and all three of us manage to board—my dog, me, and J.J. (in that order)—before the doors close.

We sit down. J.J. stares out the window for a while. Then he asks: And what happened to Jakob?

I can't say exactly. It was more than seven years ago. What do you think it's like when you die, he'd asked, is it like unplugging the TV? There was that last trip after I left him. He showed up at the literary festival to which I'd been invited. He lived in Bonn at the time and had driven all night with my dog in the car. I'd left her with him the week before, as always when I couldn't take care of her. He appeared in front of me one morning in the breakfast room of the hotel in Solothurn, and I didn't have the heart to ask him to leave. After my reading (my book smelled of Philipp's aftershave, Jakob understood right away. Good lord, how ridiculous this is, he said), I drove with him to my brother's in Zurich. He had to get some sleep, after all. It was our last car ride together. As usual, he named everything he saw. On that last drive, too, he constantly relayed his observations (or rather: sightings) and I could hardly stand it. I had to clench my teeth in order not to scream at him to be quiet, to finally just stop talking. Exit 48, Oftringen/Zofingen, 80 kph on wet roads, highway service area Kölliken-Nord in 500 meters, caution slippery conditions. He was so tired, he could hardly speak. He articulated the syllables slowly and with a groan as if he had been stabbed in the chest and was struggling to stay conscious despite indescribable pain. And just when I thought he was about to fall asleep mid-sentence, he sat up straight and said: Since I've no longer been driving alone, since I've had the dog with me, it's almost fun to say out loud everything I see. He had objected to my getting a dog. He didn't want her. And now she was the only one who listened to him. No wonder he didn't want to give her up. She's staying with me, he said.

J.J. looks at me disconsolately. All the green has drained from his eyes.

But as I see, not even the mutt stayed with him. That sounds so lonely, so sad. Damn, who wants to hear a story like that.

Don't worry, J.J., the story turns happy: Jakob is a TV-star. He has money, friends, and women galore.

J.J. looks at me and shakes his head. His dark curls tremble. You don't understand a thing, he says. *Next stop Schwert,* the recorded voice announces. I have to get out here, J.J. says and is gone.

My dog jumps up and wants to follow him. Here, I say, come here. Stay. She pricks up her ears, sits on her haunches, and whines. I stroke her head. OK, it's all OK. The number 13 drives on. Where it is headed is clear. *Next stop Alte Trotte.* But where am I headed? I've been back in my hometown for over a month—in search of? What? An alternative? A new start? That's not possible. I've tried often enough: running off, leaving everything behind, new city, new luck, new man, new happiness. It doesn't work. The least I can hope for is a reason to continue. But do I really need to find one? Won't everything go on and on, regardless, one way or another? Isn't the reason I've been wandering around this city for a month, poking around in the past, far from my husband, my children, my real life precisely this: that I'm not able to pull out, to simply jump off, to stop the carousel for a moment and get a clear picture of it all, so that I can decide if and when I'll climb back on and which horse I'll ride?

My eyes sting. I'm homesick. For my children, for my grand-mother, for times that are long gone and a promising future, for love, for all the people I've lost along the way. For you. For home. Even for the beautiful J.J., whom I only met last night, who sprang from my head and has now run off.

But I still have you, my girl, don't I? My dog whines and pulls toward the exit. I hold her back. Stay. Here. With me. Stay. She looks like she's thinking it over.

Keep going, we've got to keep going, I say and take out my notebook. At least I write every day. At least I can do that, with my dog nearby, at my feet: I keep writing this book and my life. Am I writing it or it me? My dog whines. And then I say some-thing to her I've never said before. I say *lie down* in English. How should she know what it means? And yet, she looks at me, stops, lies down.

The first dogs I got to know were border collies, work dogs that herd sheep. They'd been trained in Scotland and were frighten-ingly good at following commands like: *come by, steady, that'll do,* or even *lie down.* Although I never grew fond of these dogs, I admired their intelligence and their work ethic. When I finally decided to get a dog almost ten years later, it had to be a border collie (against the advice from everyone around me who all said something to the effect of: Those dogs require consistency, clarity, a sense of responsibility. Not qualities, apparently, anyone ascribed to me.). These are not dogs for beginners, one expert told me, get yourself a mixed breed. They're less susceptible to illness and friendlier. That sounded good to me. When I saw eight border collie mix puppies advertised in a free newspaper, I grabbed the opportunity, literally. One after the other, I put each of them on the palm of my hand. The second to last, all black with a white muzzle, fell asleep immediately. I'll take him.

Her, the owner said, she's a bitch.

That's an ugly word.

Well, I can't call her mistress, you're the mistress.

The correct term in German was *Betze,* but like *bicce* from Old English, it's no longer used. So there's female dog.

Mine is love-crazed, greedy, immoral, inspiring. I've been writing since she started lying at my feet. I can't bear to imagine what life will be like without her one day. *One day?* That day is not so far away. In two months, she'll be eleven. A few weeks ago, I was at the hairdresser's. Her salon is the gossip nerve center of the neighborhood. For fear she might know more about my husband's debts, his creditors, and his gambling addiction than I do, I'd not been there since early March. A lot can happen in eight months. She had gotten a new dog, the old one had had cancer. We had a nice hospice period, she said.

What did you do with him then? Buried him?

Sank, not buried, she said. I already have three dog graves to take care of, that's enough. A burial at sea. We sailed out to deep water and let him down in a body bag filled with sand. It was beautiful.

Why does this occur to me right now? *It was beautiful.* Yes, my grandmother would have liked it, too.

I sigh, but it probably isn't as becoming for me as for J.J. Night is already falling. I turn to my dog.

So, you understand English now.

She doesn't react.

Hello? Get up!

Nothing.

That'll do!

Nothing.

Come by.

Nothing.

Once a month I take her to the vet. Why does this occur to me right now? She hates it. On the way there, she's already trembling from head to tail. In the waiting room, it escalates to shuddering. At some point, I'll have taken her for the last time, but the idea that she might die in a place she never wanted to go is unbearable. Maybe the vet makes house calls? I'd rather give her the shots myself.

She lays her head on my knee.

I run through all the English commands again and how about this: sometimes it works, sometimes not.

Simon, who has been giving me shelter for a month now, is spending the weekend in the mountains. Help yourself, he told me, but I don't want to. I examine his refrigerator and kitchen shelves and abstain. I sit at the kitchen table and try to write, then take a bottle of red wine from the buffet after all and start looking for a corkscrew in all the cabinets, closets, and drawers. In vain. I put the bottle on the table.

And now?

Two possibilities: electric screwdriver or hammer. That's J.J.'s voice—but speaking with my husband's north German accent! He sits across from me, arms crossed.

J.J.! Where'd you come from?

He rolls his beautiful eyes, annoyed.

I mean, where exactly do you come from? You sound like you're from Zurich, France, most recently from Sankt Gallen, and now? You come from someplace completely different, always different. Now you sound like you're from the Nordheide.

He shrugs. You should know.

Then I'll tell you outright: J.J. my dear, you're from Buchholz. You're surprised, hunh? Am I right?

If you say so.

His bad mood is irritating me. Brief silence.

What now? I ask, and tap my fingernail against the neck of the bottle. J.J. grimaces. Horrible noise. He shudders. So are there any tools in this place?

A hammer.

I'd rather use an electric drill.

Haven't seen one around here yet, I say, and get the hammer from the kitchen cupboard. I ask: Me or you?

You, J.J. says. He helps me position the bottle so that the neck hangs over the sink. He shows me where I should hold it, where I should hit it, and advises me to hold the bottle upright immediately after hitting it so nothing goes down the drain in exactly the dialect my husband would have used. J.J. winks at me. He's a sly one. Here we go!

Oh, that didn't work. What a mess. A bit of wine swims around the mound on the bottom of the bottle. I pour it into a glass through a tea strainer. Cheers!

Hopefully you'll survive, J.J. says, the finest splinters are the most dangerous!

I drink. J.J. watches me.

It occurred to me in the tram that you're not gambling today, I say, Sunday rest?

Why do you want to know when and if I'm gambling?

When I think of last night: you seemed absent, frenzied, you were constantly excusing yourself to go around the corner and fiddle with your cell phone.

That was for other reasons, amorous ones, J.J. says.

I don't believe you.

But it's true! I've got another woman or two after me.

Another?

Yes, aside from you.

You just want to change the subject. You're like my husband. He told me for years that his manic fumbling with his cell phone was for his work.

You never thought he might be betraying you?

Yes, but it turned out that he wasn't sending messages to other women, but to bookies. Just like you!

Listen to me, says J.J., the boy from Buchholz in der Nordheide, now sounding very sure of himself: When I want to gamble without anyone knowing, I know how to do it.

I say nothing. I swallow.

How did you find out, anyway, about your husband? he asks.

I didn't. Uncle Günter called me up one day and asked what exactly our plans were for summer vacation.

It's early March, Uncle Günter, I answered, we don't have any plans yet.

But Philipp wanted to borrow five thousand euros to book your flights!

I can't believe Philipp told such a lame lie. He's actually very good at lying.

J.J. laughs. I believe it, he says, and he's had lots of practice, like every gambler! I'll tell you why your husband told such a lame lie! It's very simple: he believed it! And it was his only chance. He was in debt up to his neck, so he needed a large sum to win big. I'll bet you he believed his plan would work, that he would double his five thousand euros and double them again, that he'd be able to clear his debts and take his family on a nice vacation.

I don't bet with gamblers, J.J.

I don't get it.

You said: *I'll bet you.*

That's just something people say. J.J. stopped talking.

I look at him for a long time. Did I really put together this gorgeous face? I can't imagine. Next to his dark curls, his skin looks almost transparent, his deep green eyes gleam like polished marble, his lips are ruddy from speaking.

I think of what Philipp said when I met him: *First you build a mock-up, then the stage set.* You think about what you want, build a small model of it, then the life-size version. Done. Everyone is master of his own fate.

Does he still think this? And: Does it apply to gamblers? Despite his failures?

J.J. has followed my thoughts. He nods. Once a gambler, always a gambler, he says.

Then tell me, J.J., from a gambler to a gambler's wife: Why do you gamble?

I gave it up, forever and always.

Is that right?

You sound skeptical.

I am.

It's not easy to believe a gambler, hunh?

No. So you don't gamble anymore. I see. And why did you gamble before?

It's exciting. It's easy. You can win or lose. Life, on the other hand, is rarely simple and it's not always easy to tell if you're up or down, if you're on a roll, if you've hit the mark or are on your way straight down.

Silence. I think it over.

The furrow in your forehead looks like a deep, clean cut, J.J. says.

I nod. But a bloodless one, I reply.

I empty the glass. I don't feel any splinters or shards.

I'm going to sleep, J.J. Get lost now, I say, go on, time to go! My dog briefly cocks one ear when he goes out the door, then she falls back asleep.

I lie alone in Simon's bed and think of Philipp.

Love is not something you choose. I think of my grandmother. Of Undine, Andreas, Petrus, Jakob, Tadeusz. *The finest splinters are the most dangerous.* Are they all coming back? Does anything ever really end?

12

Beginning, again

No verticals, all scattered and lying.
—SAMUEL BECKETT, *BREATH*

I tried to tell the story without you but it won't work. You are and you remain. I can't get over you that easily. Just because I left you out doesn't mean you're gone. As long as I haven't told about you, I can't go back, I can't go anywhere, I can't get away.

For almost six weeks I've been sitting at Simon's kitchen table in Zurich and writing. By hand, even though I hate it, but my computer's at home in Hamburg, so I'm writing in graph-paper notebooks that always fill up.

I've got a photograph of my two sons with me. They're sitting in the bathtub, splashing me. I remember that I yelled *are you out of your minds* at them and it was if I'd given them a command to scoop water at me by the handful. They screamed with delight, I screamed in outrage *the camera's for shit now*. For shit, for shit! They both howled and didn't calm down until they were shivering with cold because there was hardly any water left in the tub. When I look at the picture, I can hear them, see them screaming. I hear them laughing, see them shivering, even crying because, in the end, I pulled the stopper out and lifted them out of the tub.

But most of all I see you. And me. How we sit in the tub together and say *no, no Mommy, we're not coming out, we want to stay in here forever.* And the water's warm, and when we pee in it, it gets even warmer. Luckily, our big brother, who said that you'll be paralyzed if you go in the tub, isn't there and so we go whenever we can. We believe our big brother, we're afraid. It's deliciously frightening, when you go. You hold it briefly, the stream, your breath, time, fear—and then? I can still move! Look! And you? We got away with it, one more time, we're home free, we did it.

He looks just like you, the little one. It's crazy. This child absolutely wants to come into this world, the gynecologist had said. It's been three years since I got pregnant, one month after my miscarriage. And a few weeks after that, in the morning on New Year's Day, blood in the toilet bowl, I knew what it meant, didn't believe it, instead I believed: *this child absolutely wants to come into this world,* and I was right. How wonderful that you're here, I said, when he arrived, battered and blue, and looked at me with his little mole eyes. One was blood-red, the left one, a blood vessel has burst during delivery. For weeks it didn't seem to want to heal. But then, all of a sudden, the baby was bewilderingly beautiful. Pink, smooth, blue-eyed. Where did he get those blue eyes? We all have dark eyes, my husband, our firstborn, and I. Where did he get those blue eyes? They're your eyes.

We took care of one another, even back then, when you were two and I was four, the same age as my children are now, and took turns peeing in the bathtub. I took care of you, the middle one of the little one, you of me, the little one of the middle one. Took care that the big one didn't catch us going in the tub, took care that he didn't hold us under water too long. Took care that no one caught us licking the wrinkled soles of each other's feet after the bath, before going to bed, and we laughed so hard when we did that, we cried.

Later, when we no longer went in the tub, we never let each other out of sight when we went swimming in the lake. You were with your friends, I was with mine. People drowned every year and the spot where our swimming area was located was considered especially dangerous. The shore fell away steeply, there was talk of underground caves, of unpredictable currents that would drag you into them if you swam too deep underwater. Be careful, our mother said, watch out for each other is what we understood.

The swimming area was at the bottom of a hill. You could look down at the swimmers from the upper sunbathing lawn and see not just their heads but their entire bodies in the dark green water. You could follow their movements in the water, could see if they sank gradually or thrashed about because: before someone drowns, he usually has cramps, the lifeguard told us, and: when someone's floundering, he needs help.

I didn't let you out of my sight and sometimes, when you and your friends got rowdy and dunked each other underwater, I got so worked up I wanted to slap you. You just laughed at me. But when I swam out or jumped from the raft again and again with my friends, I would see you standing on the upper lawn, watching, even after you said, whatever you want to do.

Once someone really did drown. I was watching him closely at the time. At eleven-years-old, I'd never seen someone like that. He's Tunisian, people said, he lives with Mrs. Rindlisbacher, she brought him back from vacation, though he could be her son. He lay on the raft and glistened in the sun. He helped my friend and me lift our inflatable mats onto the raft as we threw them into the water and jumped onto them again and again. He stretched out his hand, pulled us up, laughed with us, and even, after a while, started pushing us off the raft just before we were about to jump, again and again. I forgot you for him, forgot to keep an eye on you, forgot so completely that I didn't even know if you were still there. At some point, the Tunisian dived off the raft and swam out to sea with strong, quick strokes. Suddenly he raised an arm and shouted something no one understood. Help, my friend and I translated on the raft, and a few swimmers looked at us in astonishment, others with irritation, we didn't need any help. Out there, we screamed, don't you see, out there! The lifeguard dived into the water, T-shirt, whistle, and all, but he was too slow. Get the scuba diver, he shouted before even reaching the Tunisian, who had just gone under.

Because of the hill, the helicopter landed in the middle of the shore road, and traffic was blocked. All was quiet. We gathered around the paramedics and watched the emergency doctor in silence as he pushed on the dead man's chest with all his body weight. A gush of water came out, a gush of blood, nothing more. You slipped your hand into mine and squeezed. We got home late for dinner and mother scolded us. You looked at me, we didn't say anything and were sent to bed without dinner.

I call home. My mother-in-law answers. Oh, it's you, she says, I can't talk right now, we're making cookies, why don't you call—
There's crackling on the line.
Mama?
Hey, little one, is that you? How are you?
Making cookies, bye!
Hello? He had hung up. I call again, after four rings the answering machine clicks on and I hear my own voice saying there's no one home. I hang up. I think of our last conversation a few days ago.
Me: I love you.
The little little one: Love you too.
Me: Bye!
The little little one: Bye!
Me: Hang up!
The little little one: Hang up!
Me: One, two, three!
The little little one: One, two, three!
Me: And now hang up!
The little little one: Hang up!
And so on. We just couldn't let go. Until my husband took the receiver and pressed the red button. The last thing I heard was a long, loud scream of protest. And today? *Making cookies, bye!* I would have liked so much to talk with him longer. He has your eyes. Your big round blue eyes and long black eyelashes. Your calm, wise gaze, which I can feel on me now, even when I close my eyes. In fact, I only feel it properly when I close them. It's there, it

envelops me, so completely, so soothingly and reassuringly, sur-
rounding me like a warm bath. You haven't looked at me like that
for a long time, brother.

I've been writing since you left. I thought I'd start every book
with you since you're at my beginning.

Beginning. Beginning again with you. Every book with you. In the
beginning was the word. At my beginning, there's you.

I'm ending this book with you. To finish it. So I can finally go.
So I can go back and begin again.

When you were dying—twenty years ago, now!—when I
moved in with you, into your hospital room, which I only left
when you left this world, my lover betrayed me. On those nights
when I lay next to you in a narrow hospital bed just like yours, listening to your breathing, he went to my friend's place. That's how
I picture it. Maybe she came to him, to our apartment, but that
was more than I could imagine and so I never did and I still don't.
Though I actually do. This very second. As soon as you write
something down, an image appears, dammit. Petrus and Katrin,
Katrin and Petrus. It's grabbing at me, the image. I catch it and
hold onto it tight. That it still gets to me after twenty years! Men
can't manage alone, my grandmother said. I just shook my head.
He wasn't alone! I wasn't gone, just in the hospital, Petrus often
came to visit during the day, he just couldn't stay there overnight!

So he was alone—at night! my grandmother insisted.

No, Granma, I said, no, I can't understand and I can't forgive
him.

Then let him go, if you can, she said. She said it as if she didn't
believe I could. How right she was. Although I broke up with him
soon after, to this day I haven't really been able to let Petrus go
and the reason, I think, is that he was there when you died, saw
you take your last breath, your last cry, your last gasp. You didn't
die at night when Petrus was at Katrin's, or Katrin with him,
no you passed away on a bright spring morning, on a Saturday
twenty years ago. I can't let go of Petrus because I don't want to

let go of you. Because I don't want you to go.

Hey, assholes, get over here, I'm dying! I don't think you meant us. But we were the two assholes who heard you call, we were there. Passed away peacefully surrounded by family? No, that's not how things went. It was violent. You weren't ready, you wouldn't accept it, you weren't nearly that far gone. You fought, you yelled, you cried and screamed. And I held you and screamed *I love you* back at you, in the Swiss dialect of our childhood, even though there's no expression for it in our dialect, we've only got *I like you*, and not *I love you*, and since then I've sworn off this completely inadequate, scandalously bumbling dialect. Since then I've spoken stage German, a language that doesn't come from anywhere in particular and is at home everywhere, that isn't familiar or foreign, with clear alternatives and clear limits, imprecise, indifferent to particularities, but useful in general and effective on the whole.

I never talked with you about what you wanted *after*. I was too cowardly for that conversation. Our big brother had it with you. He said you told him that every drop of water travels around the world once and you wanted your ashes to be thrown into the lake, our lake, that actually is a river, and from there they would begin the journey. Into the lake and around the world.

I have one more picture with me, next to the one of my sons in the bathtub: the postcard of St. Christopher, the patron saint of travelers, the postcard Petrus bought for me in Mistail on our first New Year's Eve twenty years earlier, at the end of our hike through the snow that I ended up doing in my socks because the borrowed boots were so tight I couldn't walk in them, after which my feet froze to the point where I couldn't walk without shoes either. Because of a heavy snowfall, we strayed off the path. When we finally reached the church in Mistail, we wanted to sit in the front pew, take a load off our feet, and look at the seven-meter-tall St. Christopher until our feet thawed enough for us to walk home. But the church was closed on that last afternoon of the year.

When I was given that postcard, you were still alive. You had one round of chemotherapy behind you. I'm not going to die that easily, you said. It was your last New Year's. I've been carrying the postcard around with me since the beginning of the year that will soon come to an end, ever since that January evening when I searched for Petrus's name and learned that he was no longer alive. That he had jumped to his death. That he let himself fall, in a snowstorm, into the void. Almost a year, then, since I've been carrying St. Christopher around with me. Until now. Usually it's the other way around, St. Christopher does the carrying.

He was, legend has it, a giant. His appearance frightened everyone he met. In the Orthodox Church, he's often depicted with a dog's head. I particularly like that idea, even if it's a result of a mistranslation: instead of *canaaneus* (Canaanite), they'd apparently understood *caninus* (canine). In any case, there is general agreement that St. Christopher worked, in order to please God, as a ferryman without a ferry. He himself was both boat and harbor, he carried travelers on his enormous shoulders and carried them through the deep, raging water to the other shore. With him, you were in good hands. He's usually shown with a long walking staff and the Christ child on one shoulder, but rarely in the water because then the most you could see would be his head and shoulder (or possibly just a raised arm, holding the child), not more than that: he'd have no body. And because his appearance was terrifying but also warded off death, Petrus had explained to me, he was understandably always depicted life-sized and in all his splendor so that he could do his work with full power and chase death away, force it back into the beyond, make sure it didn't seize anyone. At least not anyone who was under St. Christopher's protection. A journey with St. Christopher would never lead to death. To travel with him meant to stay alive.

Petrus was very tall and it's easy for me to picture my dog's head on his shoulders. That's how I see him now. Mostly gray, his sharp muzzle pointing toward the sky. With an endlessly long torso, a very straight back that seemed almost stiff and to have thousands of vertebrae, and with steeply sloping shoulders that at first glance don't look capable of bearing anyone, not even a child, especially not one as heavy the Christ child who, after all, bears the weight of the world.

I lifted my little little one onto the shoulder of the dog-headed Petrus-Christopher, my little boy with your eyes, your round blue eyes. I zoom in until the image only shows these eyes looking at me, calm, knowing, steady. I only have eyes for these eyes. Your eyes. Let me be spellbound and carried away by them.

It wasn't a river, it was a mountain stream and the one who carried you was called Toni. He was our ski instructor. I couldn't ski well but you could. Nonetheless, year after year we were put in the same class. It was always the same scene, just different hats and jackets every year. You in front, me following. I don't care about the others. Or about Toni. I hang onto you as onto a locomotive. I don't pay attention to anything but your track, I don't try to do anything but follow. Everyone comes down sooner or later, Toni says, the only question is how. I let him talk. It has nothing to do with me. I know how I'll get down: by hanging onto you. At the start of the annual week of ski school, Toni tries to teach me something. By Wednesday, at the latest, he gives up and ignores me for the rest of the week. He only talks to you, if at all, and that's fine with me. I feel like he's addressing me, too, that's just fine. And you? Every year I become a little more embarrassing for you. It doesn't escape me, but as long as you don't shake me off, I'll hang on. On Friday, Toni announces: Real skiers don't need lifts, the real ones climb. We already know that. Friday is touring day and on Fridays we always climb on foot, in a row, skis on our right shoulders, supporting ourselves on our poles on the left. Toni in front, you second, then me, staring at the back of your neck. On top, Toni hands around his thermos, the peppermint tea is hot and sweet, here we go, everyone gets three gulps, don't screw around! And Toni counts out seven three times, then the thermos is empty and we're off. You plow your way down the slope in big, sweeping curves, the snow is heavy and wet, spring snow, I stick to your heels, you pick up speed, tighten your curves, go faster and faster and speed straight down, and me with you, then you fall. It's a miracle that I don't follow you in the decisive moment but veer sharply left and so, luckily, don't crash right into you. You keep sliding on your stomach, your bindings don't release, your skis hang rigid and unwieldy on your feet, catch, dig in, and wrench your legs. When you finally come to a stop, you can no longer stand and can no longer walk.

Toni carried you piggyback. You had to hold onto to him yourself because Toni had his hands full, your skis in one hand, both of your poles in the other. No choking, Toni yelled. You grabbed him with both arms, your legs dangled loosely, they wouldn't obey you anymore. I skied behind Toni, but not the way I followed you. I looked for my own track. We came to a small ravine with a stream at its base, swollen with so much water from the melting snow—it was March—that we couldn't cross it. Toni carried you over first and when he stood in the middle of the stream with you on his back, you turned your head toward me and I looked into your blue eyes. Then you winked the way I'd only ever seen grown-ups wink, you winked at me.

My two little boys just called. Because they can't dial any number on their own, I assume my husband helped.

Are you coming? the little little one asked.

When, when are you coming? I heard the big little one call out.

Are you coming? the little little one asked again.

When, when! his big brother yelled.

Yes, I'm coming, I answered, I'm coming now. Now.

The train is too expensive. The ticket here cost as much as I have to spend on groceries each month. Should I try hitchhiking like I used to way back when? In two hours it will be dark. If I stand on the side of the highway with my dog—who would give us a ride? To score, the two of us need daylight. In the dark, people might take us for dirty, lice-ridden, and squalid. In daylight, on the other hand, people see, they can sense that how well-groomed, polite, and entertaining we are. In daylight, everyone would pick us up. But I can't wait until daybreak. I ask around about ride-sharing possibilities. First he says no, then he says yes, the young man who wants to drive to Hamburg tonight *to party*. No, I'm not taking any dogs with me, absolutely not. A quarter of an hour later, he has changed his mind: Yeah, OK, then with the dog. We agree to meet at seven at the gas station on Hohlstrasse near the Europa Bridge.

Well, the ride's taken care of. What do you say to that, brother? I'm going home! The single golden Christmas tree ornament that Simon hung over the kitchen table as a token of the holidays catches my eye. It dangles from the ceiling on a nylon thread, ripped out of context, a ball, round and meaningless. I've already bumped it with my head several times when standing up. Now it mirrors my face back at me in black and gold: essentially a mouth, two nostrils, two eyes, two eyebrows, and between them, vertical, a deep wrinkle.

I was twelve when you first noticed it, that furrow in my brow. It was a brilliant winter day, we sat across from each other in the gondola, I was squinting, blinded by the sun and snow. What have you got there? you asked startled.

My surprise at your question wiped away the furrow. You laughed. You looked like a slash just now, you said.

Now the Christmas tree ball throws the furrow back at me, the wrinkle that has eaten its way into my forehead and refuses to leave even when I'm not dazzled or thinking hard.

Did you just say you think it's good? Was that a comment on my wrinkle—unlikely!—or an answer to the question I almost forgot again?

Silence. I have to give the answer myself.

How about this: I'll write myself a happy ending right here and now. For us, for my husband Philipp and me, then I'll go home and play it out. Philipp always says: Make a plan, then it will work. When you know what you want, you can live for it. A happy ending foretold. Now, when it's nearing the end, I tremble as I write, tremble as if with excitement, wrap myself up in Simon's quilt, but it doesn't help, I sit at the kitchen table with fluttering hands, the pen twitches.

Nothing occurs to me. I don't know how to write a positive ending. I'm afraid that at best I could only manage under the pen name Phyllis Plank, if I went outside myself, if I turned into my husband and could tap into his sense of confidence (an exchange I'd be happy to make for my sense of insecurity). It would be worth a try. I remember a dream in which I found myself with the bottom half of his body. From the navel down, I was him. I looked down at his feet. There was a wild throbbing in my legs, my buttocks, my—oh God!—penis, it flooded through me so powerfully, with such force, such life, that I only had one wish: that I would stay this way. That I would remain as much myself, as him. Amazed and throbbing. Full of wonder and desire. I don't know why but the first thing I want to do when I get home is take a family picture. With a self-timer, so that we're all in it. One of us is running, and it's not me.

I pack the picture of my sons in the bathtub and the St. Christopher card in my bag. I don't have any other luggage. I close the zipper. I love you, I think at that moment, in dialect.

After your death, I had to leave. Three weeks later, in June, I had to take an entrance exam for the Theater Academy in Salzburg and was actually admitted to it for the winter semester, though how that could have happened was inconceivable since I was in no state to recite lines much less perform. I only had the summer to earn money. I worked in the cafeteria of the Department of Transportation. Petrus didn't want to hear about my grief or about my upcoming departure. He set off on his own, to visit his brother in Canada. I believe Petrus made a few escape attempts at the time. First with Katrin, then to Canada. He wanted to escape the unhappiness. I'm still amazed that he did follow me to Salzburg after all. I'm amazed that I'm the one who ended our relationship.

My dog pricks up her ears. Simon has come home. He sees me sitting there wrapped in his quilt. He smiles. I snap my notebook shut. I'm going, I say.

As far as I'm concerned, you can stay, he says in his deep voice and it sounds as serious as everything he says. He adds, stay, stay.

I know. Thank you. Will you come visit me in Hamburg?

No, he replies.

I know, I think to myself.

We smile at each other.

I walk to the meeting point through the drifting snow with my dog. Her shaggy black fur is white. Snowflakes fall, depending on their wetness, as fast as a person walks. She pulls, I have to hurry to keep up. Luckily I've learned how. This time I'm wearing proper shoes, sturdy boots, not high-heeled pumps like before. These boots are made for walking. I've learned how to walk.